# A Brisket,
# a Casket

# A Brisket, a Casket

## Delia Rosen

**KENSINGTON PUBLISHING CORP.**
http://www.kensingtonbooks.com

*Dedicated to three whose memories
most especially brought this book to life:
Uncle Jack, Harry Burke,
and Noni Kosinski*

# Chapter One

"Hey, watch it. Ya'll almost knocked over my babka!"

"Did not."

"What you mean, Jimmy? I *saw* you bump the babka. Makes you the second person tonight."

"There you go again. A bump's a whole 'nother thing from knockin' it over. Besides, how come you're only on *my* case if somebody else did it too?"

"'Cause you're the one's here right now. And the one who ought to know better."

"Since when's ignorance an excuse, Newt?"

"Never mind. Bump my babka before the dough rises, you might as well knock it to the floor. Ain't nobody wants a flat babka."

"Saying that's true, for argument's sake. If it already got bumped twice on that there counter, maybe you should think about makin' some kinda change."

"Like what?"

"Like puttin' put your babkas someplace else."

"Like where?"

"Like anyplace except where they block the way to my machine . . ."

Turning from my office stairs—they were in the kitchen near its swing doors—I stared at the roast pig that should have been a pastrami and tried to ignore my bickering staffers. Newton Trout was the restaurant's head cook and baker. Jimmy DuHane was my dishwasher. Their nonstop arguments could be annoying at the best of moments, and I was a certified wreck.

I'm Gwen Silver née Katz, owner of the only Jewish deli in Nashville. It's named Murray's, after my dear, late uncle, Murray Katz, the illustrious Swami of Salami, who'd bought the place for a song thirty years ago and made it a Tennessee two-stepping success. When he left the business to me after his recent death, I'd been living in my native New York and was sure I wouldn't want any part of it. But sometimes things happen to make "sure" go out the window with . . . well, whatever else you toss. In my case, it was a twenty-four-karat gold Tiffany wedding band that I'd contentedly worn for half a decade.

Long story, details to come. Right now, I was too horrified by the stuffed pig on the counter in front of me to grit my teeth about my ex-husband Phil, who I suppose could be considered the pig I left behind.

Not that my present company wasn't a quality hog. Cooked to a deep golden brown, glazed to perfection, it lay on a platter of romaine lettuce with a bright red apple in its mouth, redder cherries for eyes, and seedless watermelon wedges tucked under its outstretched forelegs like fruity sofa cushions. Though larger and plumper than my new cat Southpaw, it had little piggy ears that curled exactly the way hers did when she was getting set to torment Mr. Wiggles, the elder of my two feline hell-raisers.

The difference being that the tips of the pig's ears were crisp.

Thankfully, I'd never seen Southpaw's ears with crispy tips. In fact, the image was almost upsetting enough to trigger a cigarette craving in me. Not that it took much.

"Hey, Nash . . . the kid fetch the pastrami yet?"

I tore my eyes from South—um, the roast hog. "Nash" was short for Nashville Katz, a nickname I'd kind of acquired with the restaurant. More on that later too. Promise.

As I turned toward the kitchen's swing doors, I saw that Thomasina "Stonewall" Jackson had poked her head in from the dining room amid a blast of karaoke music, her sprayed, soaring bubble of hair almost colliding with the upper door frame.

Thom's hair is a metallic bluish gray color that matches the restaurant's old-fashioned tin ceiling. I mention this because it's wise to remember that *she* describes it as snow-white, and says the poofing effect makes it look like a "yummy vanilla parfait." Anyone who differs might want to think twice about going public.

"Luke hates when you call him a kid," I said.

"Well, I hate when people cuss, and you do more of that than a cowhand with saddle itch."

"Who's cursing? Did you hear me curse?"

"Night's still young. And besides, the *kid* ain't here."

I made a face. Thomasina had been my uncle's powerhouse manager forever. To know her was to love her. Well, okay, I'm full of it. She might've come within a half mile of tolerable on the best of days. Like when the sky was full of sunshine, my hair was relatively tame, and I weighed in at 135 *before* breakfast. And when I won at least fifty bucks on the scratch Lotto. *And* the guy who cashed my ticket was an ultimate blue-collar hunk.

"Luke phoned from the airport a few minutes ago." I wobbled my cell phone in the air. "He had a problem at the baggage claim."

"What's the pastrami doin' in baggage claim? I thought it came on a super-duper air cargo flight?"

"It did."

"Then why ain't it at the cargo terminal?"

"Good question," I said. "All I know is there was a mix-up somewhere. And that the pastrami wound up on the carousel."

"At a *passenger* terminal."

"Right."

"With people's suitcases?"

"I guess."

"You guess? Did the pastrami land or not?"

I shrugged. "Luke spotted it on the conveyor belt and pushed his way through the crowd. But it got carried back around behind the wall before he could grab it."

"And then what?"

"That was the last I heard from him."

"So you *don't* know that it got here."

"I told you, Luke saw it. They packed it in a special cooler."

Thomasina looked skeptical. "They" meant the Star Deli in Burbank, California, and she mistrusted anyone or anything beyond the Tennessee border. Never mind that I'd only phoned in a long-distance pastrami 911 because our local meat distributor messed up my order, which I'd in turn only placed after our online corporate catering orders had mysteriously gotten zapped into cyber limbo. The same-day air delivery had cost ten times more than I would take in for the next *three* days, but the next best option had been FedEx overnight, and that would've gotten the pastrami to me too late.

"The kid ain't back soon, we go with the hog," Thomasina said.

"We can't," I said, shaking my head. "There's no hog in Jewish cooking."

"Ain't no servin' dairy with meat either. But we got Ruben sandwiches and cheese blintzes on the menu."

I sighed. Suddenly Thomasina, who ran her Baptist congregation's annual bake and craft fair, and led the local chapter of the Women's Inter-Church Curling League, had also become a certified *expert* on kosher dietary law. Of course, it was an open secret that Thom had been carrying on with my uncle for over two decades when she wasn't singing gospel hymns. After spending half her life around the deli as his manager and play pal, she probably knew much more than I did about the technical distinction between strictly kosher cooking and our kosher-style dishes—an expertise I hadn't needed while ordering at Upper East Side sushi bars or poking through designer apparel collections at Saks Fifth Avenue. Back when I could afford to splurge on such luxuries.

Still, only her anxious expression convinced me she wasn't covertly testing my deli acumen. So what if I owned the place? I'd felt on probation with Thom since the day I first set foot in Nashville.

"Nope, uh-uh, forget it," I said. "Hog is out. The idea of serving it here would give poor Uncle Murray a heart attack . . . if one hadn't already killed him."

She stared at me a second. Then her features softened.

"Your uncle never tired of complainin' about these catered affairs bein' more trouble than they were worth," she said. "But he knew when push was on its way to shove, hon. Better a stuffed pig on the table than a bunch of starved Southern men around it."

*Hon?* What had brought that on? I felt like a fly buzzing around sugary bait. But never mind, she'd gotten me there. Kosher Karaoke night was a tradition at the delicatessen, and we couldn't blow the first since our grand reopening. Especially with Yakima Motors, the latest Japanese automotive company to move its headquarters to Nashville, having booked a catered dinner to celebrate their new partnership with the area's leading dealership chain, Sergeant's Cars and Trucks.

Somehow, though, I had to make some wiggle room.

"We've got, what, six tables of five for the Yakima affair?"

Thomasina nodded.

"And how's it break down far as orders?" I asked

"Twenty-one pastrami sandwiches. Twelve corned beef. Plus seven sliced briskets in gravy. Well, make it eight briskets. But one's yours."

I did some quick first-grade math. Minus my dinner plate, that totaled up to the full party of thirty.

"How long can you stall? Serving the main courses, that is."

"I don't know." Thomasina scrunched her forehead. "The briskets are being served."

"The *rest* of the dinners then."

She expelled a breath. "We wait much longer'n ten minutes, stomachs are gonna rumble—"

"Stretch it to twenty minutes. Roll out some extra chopped herring and lox platters. With plenty of bagels. And the Fiddler's Fried chicken wings. More trays of Smoky Mountain potato knishes too . . . everybody loves those knishes." I paused. "The airport's only a fifteen-minute drive from here. Maybe Luke hasn't called back because he's on his way. Our partiers can nosh on appetizers to their hearts' content till he—"

My *binking* cell phone interrupted me. I dreaded when it binked rather than sounded a musical ringtone. A bink meant I had an incoming text message, most of which included shortcuts I couldn't understand.

Glancing at the display, I saw the message was from Luke and opened it. It read:

### PSTRMI OK. TRFC JM I-40. @DLSON. GFN ... CYA!

I stared at the screen in anxious confusion.

"What's wrong?" Thomasina said.

"This." I showed her the message. "I got the 'pastrami okay' part. I *think* I got the 'traffic jam on Interstate Forty' part. You understand the rest?"

Thomasina shook her head. "I once tried texting my daughter and wound up joinin' a nudist colony outside Crossville."

I frowned, looked around at Newt and Jimmy. They were still squawking about the babka.

"Hey, guys, c'mon. Give it a rest!" I held up the phone for them. "I got a text from Luke and need a translation. Either of you want to take a shot?"

They stopped barking at each other long enough to glance at the display. Newt's round, bearded face was vacant. So was Jimmy's under his white mushroom of a cook's cap. After a moment, they went right back to their tiff, not even bothering to answer.

"Crap," I said, pivoting toward the kitchen doors.

"Told you the night was young."

*Thomasina.* I wasn't in the mood.

"Crap isn't a curse word," I said. "If I wanted to use a curse word, I'd say *bullsh*—"

"Where you going?" she interrupted before I could defile her sensitive buttercup ears.

"Agnes Jean," I muttered under my breath. "Maybe A.J. can help me."

I pushed through the doors into the dining room and found the place hopping, the mingled, mouth-watering scents of knishes, kasha varnishkes, and other delicacies filling the air. They instantly comforted me the way they had when I was a young girl visiting Uncle Murray—before he went off chasing one dream only to find another.

A.J. was serving beers near the movable karaoke stage, her back to me, her Appalachian forest of blond hair spilling over her shoulders. Tonight, she had on a huggy midriff blouse and low-rider jeans, the bare skin between them displaying most of a colorful tattoo that ran from just above her waist down to parts unknown. It looked sort of like an extraterrestrial serpent with butterfly wings, and undulated lengthwise as she swung her hips to the beat of "Oh Lonesome Me," which right now was being giddily mauled by one of the Japanese auto executives.

I went up the aisle to A.J. and tapped her shoulder.

"Yippee!" she said, turning to face me.

"Yippee?" I asked.

She flashed an enormous lipstick smile, her drink tray in hand. "These here folks are having a blast! We're back in business!"

I thought worriedly about the absent pastrami and didn't comment.

"A.J., can you please read this for me?" I said,

showing her the text message on my phone. "It's from Luke."

She studied the backlit display.

"Done," she said.

I looked at her. With A.J., it was best to be specific.

"Aloud," I said. "I need you to read it aloud."

She smiled at me some more.

"Sure," she said. "Luke says the pastrami's okay."

Which I'd already managed to figure out.

"And that there's a traffic jam on the interstate."

Check again, I thought.

"Luke's at Donelson Pike," A.J. went on.

"Where's that?"

"Right outside the airport. It's the local road into town . . . guess he figures to go around the tie-up."

I felt my panic subside a bit. Out the corner of my eye, I saw a member of the Sergeant contingent grab the mike onstage. A second later, "Oh Lonesome Me" ran less than seamlessly into "Mammas, Don't Let Your Babies Grow Up to Be Cowboys."

"And the rest?"

A.J. looked clueless.

"Of Luke's *message*," I said.

"Oh, right," she said. "He wrote 'gone for now' . . ."

"Ah-hah."

"Then CYA."

No kidding, I thought. "Meaning?"

She hesitated, leaned forward confidentially, and whispered, "Cover your ass."

It was panic redux time. "Cover my . . . *why?*"

A.J. shrugged. "I don't know. Maybe 'cause the

speed limit on the pike's just forty-five miles an hour. You should call Luke and find out."

I blinked. Under normal circumstances, I was a methodical, rational person. Back in my old life, I'd made a successful *career* out of being methodical and rational. How could I not have thought to simply one-touch Luke's number and ask him what was up?

I punched it into the phone, waited. He answered after three rings.

"Gwen!"

"Luke, where are you—?"

"In my wheels with the pastrami," he said. "Baby's safe n' sound—ridin' shotgun next to me."

This time I guarded against becoming too reassured. "How long till you're here?"

"Oh . . . I'd say about three minutes."

"Don't joke."

"I ain't," Luke said. "It took some doin' . . . I got a police escort."

"A *what*?"

"Can't talk anymore," he said. "Tell the kitchen boys to have their carvin' knives ready. Bye!"

I stood grinning as he broke the connection. Luke wasn't just a good waiter. He was my knight in skintight blue jeans.

I finally let my relief settle in.

"Everything okay?" A.J. was watching my face.

"Great," I said. "Seriously great."

She beamed a smile at me, nodded toward the stage. "Seems things're picking up all ways round. Will you look who's singing *now*?"

I looked. Buster Sergeant himself had taken the

stage, dressed in black from his gleaming ostrich Western boots to his enormous ten-gallon hat. Tall, square-jawed, and looking every inch the successful car and truck entrepreneur, he'd launched whole hog—pardon the expression—into a rousing version of "King of the Road."

It didn't take him long to impress his audience, especially the Japanese honchos, some of whom had joined in the fun by wearing Buster-esque cowboy hats that looked way too big for their heads. They cheered. They clapped enthusiastically. As he went on singing, they drummed their palm on their tables and raised their beer mugs to toast him.

Meanwhile, A.J. stood beside me swinging her hips to the music. I saw a male customer to my right check out her dipping tat and almost told her to CYA, but decided against it. She got the best tips in the house, and more power to her.

"I better go take some more drink orders," she said, motioning to the Yakima group. "Got a hunch they'll want refills before too long—"

She abruptly stopped talking, her eyes glued to the karaoke stage. As the song built to its climax, Sergeant had whipped his hat off his head with a dramatic flourish, and then spread his arms wide for the final refrain.

*"I'm a man of means by no means, King of the roooa. . . ."*

He'd been holding the word *road* for about four seconds when he coughed.

Once.

Then, his arms still outstretched, he suddenly

dropped the hat and fell straight backward with a hard, loud crash.

I gaped at the stage. Some of the Japanese guys had stood up to applaud, figuring the fall was part of his act. But I didn't like the look of things. Nope, nope, not at all.

Maybe it was my imagination, but I thought I'd seen Buster's face turn eggplant-purple before he went down.

I stayed rooted in place for an endless moment. Buster wasn't moving, another bad sign. Dimly now, I heard a siren howl somewhere in the background.

A.J. looked at me in growing dismay. "You figure an ambulance could've come this quick?" she asked.

I shook my head.

"Actually," I said, "I think it's the pastrami."

# Chapter Two

"How can you tell me nobody goes in or out, Red?" Luke asked the aptly carrot-topped cop blocking the kitchen entrance. "You realize I got perishable meat over here?"

"If I didn't, you'd still be stuck in traffic," the cop said. Arms folded across his chest, he nodded sideways toward the karaoke stage, where several other uniformed policemen had gathered around the sprawled body of Buster Sergeant. "Problem's the perishable meat over *there*. And he ain't packed in dry ice same's your corned beef—"

"It's a pastrami," Luke said.

"Whatever."

"There's a difference."

"Like I said, whatever." Red frowned. "I swear, you ain't never changed."

"Huh?"

I watched the cop uncross his arms.

"Been spoiled rotten since you were this high," he said, holding his palm about three feet above the floor. "You can gripe till the cows come home or boo-hoo-hoo about it in one'a your cryin' songs, but you ain't gonna get your way just 'cause—"

"Hold on there. Was that a knock on my song-writin'?"

The cop shrugged again. "I'm just sayin' you'll have to wait for us to get done."

"And when's that gonna be?"

"Whenever it is, cousin."

It was Luke's turn to frown. He hefted the carton he'd schlepped in from outside the restaurant. "Talk about cows . . . the hunk I got in my hands weighs more'n thirty pounds before the ice. And costs over five hundred dollars. That about right, Nash?"

He looked over at me. Red the cop's eyes followed. While I wasn't thrilled to find myself in their trajectory, I knew Luke needed some backup. The carton was heavy, sure. But he was arguing at least partly on my behalf.

"We spent exactly five hundred fifty-four dollars on the pastrami," I said. "Plus another thousand and change on shipping."

Red stared at me. "Mercy," he said.

"Yeah, well," I said. "I definitely didn't get any when it came to the price."

Red shook his head sympathetically, but didn't budge from in front of the kitchen's double doors. I could see Newt and his staff behind the doors, crowding to peer through their rectangular glass panes. They were stuck there on the other side, having been instructed to stay put by the cops.

"I truly apologize for this inconvenience, ma'am." Red expelled a breath, tipped his head toward the karaoke stage again. "But there's a lot goin' on, as y'all can see."

That I could. Crouched over Buster Sergeant's body were two paramedics who'd dashed in from an EMT wagon moments after the squad cars showed up. A cop stood by the stage watching them work, with more uniformed policemen crowding the front of the restaurant—among them a tall, handsome officer with a pad and pencil talking to A.J. and Thomasina over by the register. Another pair of cops had hustled the members of the Yakima-Sergeant's Cars and Trucks party toward a corner booth for interviews. The Japanese corporate types were still wearing cowboy hats that were mostly too large on them. I noticed they'd spun halfway around their heads and in some cases dipped low over their eyes. Or both.

From the look of things, not to mention the sheer number of policemen, you would've thought somebody had gotten murdered—and that confused me. Buster was singing up a storm when he collapsed. Everyone's eyes, including mine, were on him. I didn't know if he'd had a sudden heart failure, a stroke, or what, but felt he'd clearly died of natural causes. I realized that Buster was a big wheel in Nashville, no pun intended. I figured that was why a whole swarm of NMPD cruisers had come screaming up to the deli after Luke's cousin and pastrami escort, Red the cop, arrived to find him motionless onstage. But the place resembled a major crime scene, the police cars outside clogging Broadway's main drag, their roof bars flashing into the already garish neon glow of the honky-tonks to draw gawks from curious nightclubbers.

Insensitive as it might sound, I was worried about the harm that sort of attention might do to business. A customer dropping dead on my first Kosher Karaoke night—a famous customer, no less—was about the worst sort of publicity imaginable. I knew the local media would be all over the story and could almost hear the nightly news promo. *"Coming up at eleven: Main Course, Heart Attack! King of the Road Dead Ends at Murray's Deli."*

I frowned. A man had passed away in my restaurant and here I was consumed with self-interest. I felt desperately ashamed.

Okay. Maybe that's an exaggeration. But I sincerely wished Buster was alive, well, and enjoying his dinner. And I did have a desperate yearning for some comfort chocolate. My automatic grab would be a Nestlé's Crunch mini-bar from the bag up in my office, although I also had some Goo Goo clusters that my next-door neighbor Cazzie had given me to check out. Too bad the office stairs were off limits in the kitchen—an architectural quirk that had something to do with the location of a support wall and the interior redesign that had turned a decrepit century-old tavern into Murray's.

Chocolate and a smoke, I thought longingly. They went together like . . . well, chocolate and a smoke.

"Nash, you look a fright."

*Oh joy,* I thought. Thomasina had arrived to

further undermine my confidence. Was there such a thing as an anti-cavalry?

I looked around, my eyes climbing to her face. At five-foot-eight, she stood a full six inches taller than I did, making me glad she favored slip-ons with a medium-wedge heel to reduce her intimidating height advantage. Now she'd pushed over through a group of cops, leaving the officer with the notepad still talking to A.J at the front counter. Or more likely trying to score a date, since the pad was back in his breast pocket, his eyes were locked on hers, and they were swapping big, bright, cutesy smiles.

"Thanks," I said to the countenance looming overhead. "Utter catastrophes have that effect on my appearance."

A don't-get-uppity look smashed down on me. Thom had a thing for color-coordinated outfits, and tonight was wearing tan slacks with beige wedges and a sea green Indian blouse the same color as her eyes (she claimed they were her best feature). There were little iridescent white beads across the breast of the gauzy top, emphasizing what she boasted was her second best attribute.

After a long moment of gazing upon Mount Thomasina with dread and awe, I turned toward the booth where the cops had gathered the Yakima-Sergeant party. The brim of his outsized Stetson dunked way down over his nose, one of the Japanese execs stood there taking questions from a burly officer I doubted he could even see.

"Was Mr. Sergeant actin' funny or anything before he collapsed?" I heard the cop ask him.

"Yes, funny!" The exec gave a wistful smile, his mouth the only part of his face left uncovered by the hat. "He a funny, funny man."

The cop blinked, puzzled. "Think maybe you misunderstood," he said. "What I want to know is . . . did he do anything, like, out of the ordinary?"

"Yes, yes. Comedy and beautiful karaoke singing! Mr. Sergeant was total entertainment!"

I looked back at Thomasina. "This can't be real. I'm in bed with a high temperature, right? Having nightmarish hallucinations."

"That's so. I think the same fever's messing with my brain." She glanced past me toward Luke and his cousin. "You got any idea what they're tanglin' over?"

"Nobody's allowed in or out of the kitchen," I replied with a nod at Red. "He said something about preserving the integrity of the investigation."

"Investigation? What's to investigate?"

"Well, under the circumstances, I assume he meant Buster Sergeant's death . . ."

"It isn't like someone on the kitchen staff went crazy on him. The man kicked all on his own!"

"Look, you asked what's going on. And I told you. Doesn't mean I agree with it."

Thom's scowl deepened. "Red got his nerve," she said, raising her voice loud enough so he could hear. "We been takin' good care of the boys from the station for years."

Nice, I thought. *Perfect.* Antagonizing the cops was always helpful.

I felt my molars grind together as Red peered over at us from the kitchen doors.

"Thomasina, I resent that comment," he said. "None of us ever come in here expectin' special treatment."

She glowered. "That correct?"

"I'd say it is absolutely, one-hundred-percent correct."

"Well, then, I'd suggest you peek at the menu," she said. "Surprise, surprise, you'll find out egg creams *ain't* on the house."

Before things could escalate, I edged between Thomasina and the cop. "He's got his orders, Thom," I said, my back to him. "I don't see how we can get around them."

Looking disgusted, she shifted her attention from Red to Luke. "Say what you want about me bein' a prude, it's my opinion the kid's tight jeans ain't proper restaurant attire," she told me in a lowered voice. "Luke can show his package all he wants while he's shakin' his hips next door at Trudy's. But nobody comes here to get porn served with the pastrami. You really think a *waiter* ought to share that much personal information with folks?"

I gave him a hopefully inconspicuous sidelong glance, wondering if Thomasina the Pure considered her huggy Indian top any less info-packed.

"Can't see how it hurts," I said, clearing my throat. "But I don't get what that has to do with anything right now. Or am I somehow missing your point?"

Thom fixed me in a hard stare. "My *point,* so it's clear, is that in spite of Red's thick skull, I can't blame him for not takin' Luke seriously," she grunted after about ten seconds, stepping away.

"Hold it," I said. "Where are you going?"

"To give our blue-denim loverboy some help," she said. "I see no good reason for keeping those kitchen doors shut—"

"One minute, Thomasina," somebody said behind us. "That isn't for you to decide."

She paused in midstep at the sound of the unfamiliar voice. Or more accurately, unfamiliar to *me*.

We spun toward the main aisle, where I noticed a couple of things at the same time. One was the emergency techs wheeling Buster Sergeant toward the door on a gurney, a sheet pulled over his head—not a positive clinical sign. The other was the tall, lean guy approaching us in a charcoal sport jacket and tan slacks, his dark brown eyes very intent.

"Kind of you to visit, Beau McClintock," Thom said. And, yes, that was very definitely sarcasm dripping from her words. "Beau's a detective with the Metro police. And an old friend. Don't see him much these days, but he always shows up for happy occasions."

*Deee-ripping.*

He looked at her pointedly before shifting his attention to me. "How do you do, Ms. . . . ."

"Katz," I said. "Gwen Katz."

McClintock nodded. No handshake offered.

"You're the deli's new owner?" he said. "Murray's niece?"

I had a moment to look surprised as I eyed the shield on his lapel pocket.

"Right to both," I said. "Detective, we've got a horrible situation . . ."

"Yes," he said. "It's why I'm here."

I stood feeling boneheaded. *Sure, why else?*

"Beau, listen up," Thom said. "How about you just tell your officers we can open the kitchen doors?"

"Sorry, I can't," McClintock said. "A man's died in the restaurant—"

"Not officially," one of the techs pushing the gurney shouted from behind McClintock. "Officially, he's showing no vital signs."

"But you've stopped trying to resuscitate him."

"That's right."

"And covered up his face."

"Right, right."

"Meaning I can assume Mr. Sergeant isn't among the living."

"He's a stone-cold goner, you want my *unofficial* judgment." The tech and his partner were maneuvering the gurney past the front counter. "I'm just sayin', we're being technical, the coroner's got to pronounce him DOA at the hospital—"

"I hear you," McClintock said. "Thanks."

"Don't mention it," the tech shouted over his shoulder.

McClintock released a long breath, then watched as the gurney was wheeled out onto the street and loaded aboard the waiting emergency vehicle. Finally, he looked back at Thom.

"Sorry for the eruption," he said.

"That's twice you apologized since you walked in."

"I suppose."

"So when you gonna quit addin' to your *sorrys* and do right by lettin' us open the kitchen?"

He looked straight at her again. "My men still have work to do. Bottom line, nothing changes until they're finished."

Thomasina's eyes blazed with anger. I imagined their heat rays searing the tips of McClintock's ears so they crisped like those of the hog that had started off the night's assorted problems. Problems that now included one of Nashville's most prominent citizens dropping dead while performing extraordinary and beautiful karaoke at the restaurant.

But McClintock's ears didn't crisp, curl, or even slightly singe. Nor did any other visible part of his body. He just faced her in unruffled silence.

"What sort of work?" I broke in before Mount Thom could rumble again. "It isn't as if a crime was committed—"

"No one's suggesting that," McClintock interrupted.

"But if Buster died of natural causes . . ."

"No one's saying that either."

"Then what *are* you saying?"

He shot me a pointed look. "I'm not aware of any rule that says I have to explain my job to you."

"I didn't mean to be difficult . . ."

"Once again, Ms. Katz, I'm here on police work. It's unfortunate if that puts you out. But a man has died. And there's a chance we'll need samples to determine why it happened."

"Samp—you mean *food samples*?"

McClintock nodded so faintly it seemed an inconvenience. "It's important that no cooked or uncooked food leave the kitchen. The same goes for leftovers. I don't want your people disposing of anything from inside the restaurant . . . not a single table scrap."

I opened my mouth, closed it. And then just stared at him in baffled silence.

"How about this pastrami? Since technically it ain't *from* the restaurant? Being it wasn't here when Sergeant kicked the bucket."

That was from Luke, who'd apparently been preparing to jump headlong into the breach.

I looked at him. Thomasina and McClintock did too. He'd slouched forward a little from holding the heavy cooler over by the kitchen doors, where his cousin Red was still playing the role of human roadblock.

"I'll have one of my men take it to the lab for trace analysis," McClintock said.

*Trace analysis?* Luke's face was shocked—and uncharacteristically timid. I didn't blame him. He needed help explaining. The pastrami had set me back over fifteen hundred dollars.

"You don't understand," I said. "What he means is that it came from—"

McClintock snapped around to face me. "I got him the first time."

"Detective, listen, I'm not sure you did," I persisted. "See, that pastrami was really, really expensive. I flew it in all the way from Hollywood on a private jet—"

McClintock brought up his palm in a silencing gesture.

"We'll be sure to give it full red-carpet treatment," he said, and walked off without another word.

I watched him a moment, at a total loss. Then turned to Thomasina. "What the hell is *his* problem?"

She frowned.

"There goes that foul mouth again," she said.


I was in my tiny shipwreck of an office above the delicatessen looking at a framed 8x10 photo of Uncle Murray and me. Murray had hung it to the left of my desk back when it was his desk, right above a battered hardshell acoustic guitar case leaning upright against the wall. The case—a Gibson—had been there the day I arrived from New York and did nothing but take up space. But I hadn't had the heart to move it elsewhere. It reminded me too much of my uncle . . . as did the cover of an old Loretta Lynn LP beside my photo, though in a different way.

Titled "Your Squaw Is on the Warpath," it showed Loretta wearing a teensy Indian mini-dress with beaded tassels hanging over her thighs. The personalized autograph written across those same shapely bare thighs read, *"What you thinkin' about, Murray? LL."*

As if she'd needed to ask.

It was now five minutes past midnight. At around eleven-thirty, the last of the police officers and evidence techs had left the restaurant below, parading off with Ziploc bags full of table scraps and armloads of perishables from our freezers and refrigerators. My customers and serving staff had been allowed to go home long before that, and although the kitchen was no longer under cordon, Newt and Jimmy had stuck around to help Thomasina put it—and the dining room—back together again.

All the deli's horses and all the deli's men, I thought moodily.

With the cops gone, I'd stepped out onto the street for a smoke. But before I could end my latest cigarette abstinence streak at four days and counting, I'd turned back inside without lighting it and pushed through the kitchen doors, thankful the office was finally accessible again. Then I'd walked upstairs, gotten a Goo Goo cluster and Nestlé bar out of my top drawer, and set them in front of me as I sat studying their wrappers and deciding which one to greedily ingest.

I hadn't yet made my choice, but the unlit cigarette was still in my mouth. The Non-Smokers Protection Act banned smoking in Nashville's workplaces, so I couldn't light up till I left the premises. Although this was my private office, and I was the only person who actually worked in it, I'd been told that wasn't a satisfactory loophole. No sense getting shut down on a legal trifle. If Murray's was going to close, it would be in grand fashion.

The result, say, of a storm of bad publicity due to a local bigshot dying from our food. Hypothetically, of course.

I stared at the snapshot above the untouchable guitar case and reminisced, my door locked so nobody could walk in and catch me sautéing in melancholy. My dad had taken the picture at Murray's suburban home in

Hicksville, about an hour's drive from Manhattan on the Long Island Expressway. I think it was one of our family's annual Passover get-togethers. I'd been nine or ten years old, which would've put Murray in his early forties.

That was around twenty-five years ago. A long time. Still, Uncle Murray had left us too young. They say a modern person at sixty-something is equivalent healthwise to the previous generation's fifty-somethings.

Or something.

I guess Murray's leaky aortic valve hadn't gotten word of current life-expectancy trends.

In the photo, we were posing by his enormous kitchen range. Murray had pulled over a chair and lifted me onto it, and I'd knelt so I could reach the pots and pans on his stovetop as I helped him cook. Smiling as we clinked spatulas for the camera, we wore aprons he'd bought us with the slogan *"Schmutz Happens"* in front.

Cute.

I leaned back in my chair, and it squealed like a strangled monkey before clunking against a wobbly stack of cartons behind me. The boxes were heavy and full, and I hadn't yet peeled back their flaps to pore through their contents. I mentioned that the office was a wreck, right? The USS *Murray*. Although I'd cleared a lot of junk off the desktop, a memo spindle in one corner stood crammed with telephone messages in Thomasina's handwriting. Most were from Artemis Duff, my uncle's friend, longtime drummer—and accountant.

One of Murray's original band members, Artie

was one of those rare musicians who'd been grounded enough as a young man to get a college degree and a day job. He'd been dashing in and out of the restaurant for weeks, blizzards of loose paper spilling from the overstuffed ledgers he took from the office. Since we were overdue for a conversation about the tangled state of my uncle's finances, I figured I'd wait before tossing the memos, just in case the two men hadn't been caught up—a distinct possibility given Murray's chronic disorderliness. There were record books, overstuffed manila folders, and loose mounds of paperwork just about everywhere around me. A little digging had revealed some metal file cabinets, a credenza, and a couple of extra chairs beneath the jumbled mess, and I had a hunch that running a giant vacuum cleaner over the room might bare a few more pieces of furniture. Hopefully, there'd be nothing too gross decomposing among them.

Aside to public health inspectors: I jest.

The clutter wasn't my doing. It had been part and parcel of my inheritance, coming along with the restaurant downstairs. In all truth, I'd probably had enough time to straighten up the office. It had been over three months since my move to Nashville. But a whole list of to-dos took precedence . . . or was it a list of excuses?

Whatever term fit, I knew I'd get around to the unenviable task before long. I'm very structured when it comes to work, having spent almost a decade sorting out corporate books at a boutique forensic accounting firm on Wall Street. My career at Thacker Consulting was basically about clearing trails through tangled arithmetical woods, and I'd become very systematic in my professional habits. Out of necessity rather than disposition, I concede.

Housekeeping was another story, though I try to avoid slobbette status. Losing one of my cats under a pile of dirty wash would be tragic and inhumane.

A slow, thoughtful breath slipped out over the unlit cigarette in my lips. Then I tilted forward to study another picture of Murray, one I'd brought from New York and stood on the opposite end of the desk from the memo spindle. This time my chair's rickety springs made just the ittsiest bittsiest of squeaks, that's how careful I was not to further destabilize the Leaning Tower of Cartons.

The photo was professionally taken—I always thought of it as his "guitar headshot." Murray gripping the neck of a Les Paul with both hands, his shirt black with white piping and pearl snaps. Broad-nosed, full-lipped and dark complected, his male-pattern baldness hidden by a flashy white felt cowboy hat with a silver buckle and whiskey-colored edging around the brim, he could have been described as a Semitic Garth Brooks. But though he'd gone for the macho-introspective look for the shoot, there was a wicked humor in his eyes that I'd never seen from Garth.

At the bottom, in bold metallic Sharpie ink, he'd written:

*Keep Ridin' Gwennie!*
*My Heart To Yours*
*Uncle M*

My eyes lingered on the inscription. After a while, they started to sting.

"Keep ridin'," I read aloud, plucking the cigarette out of my mouth to hold it between my fingers.

I was trying. I really was. My ex-husband had scammed his investors out of their life savings even while cheating on me with a flock of silicone-accessorized pole dancers. When he got caught redhanded at both, we'd all wound up sharing the losses.

I'd been left heartbroken as well as broke. Or nearly broke. Incapable of stooping too low, Phil had secretly blown most of my personal assets along with his clients', and I'd sunk nearly every cent I had left into the condo and reopening the deli.

"I have to keep riding, Uncle Murray," I said quietly. "You know I hate feeling sorry for myself. You *know*. But maybe I do a little right now. Because another fall like the last one and not all the deli's horses or—"

I snipped off the end of the sentence, unwilling to finish it. Everyone in my family had called Murray a hopeless dreamer, but I'd always seen him as a bright, free spirit without a grain of pessimism in his bones. Someone not all the world's weight could crush.

It might have disappointed him to hear me say that *any* fall would stop me from pulling my broken pieces together and climbing back up on my horse. No matter how badly I was hurting.

I exhaled again and checked my wristwatch. Half past midnight already. The kitties would be starved for their eight-hundred-thirty-ninth absolute last meal of the day. My, how time flew when somebody croaked in your restaurant and you had trouble choosing your comfort candy.

Setting down my cigarette, I dragged a palm across my eyes and appraised the Goo Goo and Nestlé bars. Then I reached for the latter, and made a crinkly racket tearing open its wrapper. I owed Cazzie an objective review, and thought it would've been unfair to form an opinion of something new and untried in my current frame of mind.

Not that I was *too, too* upset or anything.

But the wetness on my hand from wiping my eyes gave the chocolate a weirdly salty taste as I scoffed it down.

# Chapter Three

The morning after the karaoke calamity, I was having my regular Saturday breakfast with Cazzie Watts in the abundant sunshine bathing her kitchen table. The window was wide open, its yellow lace curtains parted to admit the scent of garden lilies.

"Caz, I'm a gefilte fish out of water," I said.

"That doesn't sound good," Cazzie said. "But you know what's worse?"

"What?"

"Being a gefilte fish *in* water," Cazzie said. "Well, if by water you mean a lake or the ocean."

I looked across the table at her. For the uninitiated, gefilte fish is a type of food, not a fish per se, though the recipe does contain fish as its main ingredient. You mix ground whitefish, matzo meal, eggs, carrots, and onions together in balls or patties and poach them in seasoned broth.

Soooo . . . gefilte fish can't swim in water. Or even float. Since they're *cooked patties,* get it?

Caz's little witticism wasn't bad. Never mind that

the qualifying clause had cost her some pithiness points, it ordinarily might have gotten a half smile out of me. I couldn't manage one, however, having started the day feeling pretty cooked myself. I'd applied super-concealer to the dark, puffy bags under my eyes, and lifter cream to their droopy lids, but had no illusions about the combo making me look half as fresh as the breeze riffling the curtains. In fact, my cosmetic objective was very modest . . . say, to avoid being mistaken for a female Morlock.

"I mean it," I said after a moment. "It's like I'm totally out of my element."

"It wouldn't be the first time you had a bad night."

"But *this* time's different."

"How so?"

"When things go wrong for me, I always bounce back fast. A pre-bedtime chocolate binge followed by a few hours of optional sleep, and I'm good as new."

"And today?"

"Bounceless," I said. "Truthfully, Caz, I've started to doubt I can fit in."

"At the deli? Or are you talking about Nashville in general?"

I shrugged, spreading my hands. Technically Cazzie Watts and her family were my neighbors *outside* Nashville, our adjoining villa-style condos being located in Antioch, a small suburban town about a dozen miles southwest of the city off Highway 41.

"It's the whole deal, Caz," I said. "I'm not sure

I can cut living here. Or if I've got what it takes to run Murray's. It's awful."

She just stared at me and shook her head.

"It *isn't* awful?" I said.

"I think it's very normal considering what happened yesterday," she said.

I looked at her. Cazzie was an African American woman of about thirty-five with a nutmeg complexion, dark brown eyes, and fine, high-cheekboned features accented by a lush wedge of soft medium-length black curls. She was wearing a raspberry halter-neck blouse and faded skinny jeans of an enviously small size . . . one that would have led to a full, numbing loss of circulation in my legs had I dared try them on.

"Do you want to discuss it?" Cazzie said into the extended silence.

"Nothing to discuss," I said with the shrug that had become my all-purpose gesture of the morning.

She continued to peer across the table. Too tired for a staring contest, I lowered my eyes to the cereal boxes between us. One was Lucky Charms, her seven-year-old Cole's fave. The other was Cocoa Puffs, which his brother Jimmy, who was a wizened eight, deemed a superior product.

I had cast my lot with Jimmy. Probably the reason was my chocolate fetish. Also, I identified with the cuckoo bird mascot, since its crest kind of resembled mine before I dragged a brush through the frizz every morning.

As I turned the boxes sideways and diligently studied their nutritional ingredients, Cazzie reached over to her countertop for the newspaper and made a brief show-and-tell of its front page. The *Nashville Times* tabloid writers had been more pedestrian about slapping on their headline than I'd foreseen:

## BUSTER SERGEANT DIES AT 56
### Deli Dinner Becomes
### Auto Legend's Last Supper

"I thought maybe this was the cause of your funk," Cazzie said, holding up the paper.

I poo-poohed her suggestion with a flick of my hand. "Why'd anybody let that stupid rag of a paper bother them?"

Cazzie made a face. "Gwen . . . do you or don't you want to tell me what's wrong?"

I breathed in the naturally perfumed air from outside, exhaled. "What's wrong is that I felt irrelevant last night," I said at last. "I'm the restaurant's owner, but I might as well have been a spectator. It was like I'd stepped into a situation I didn't understand . . . and that hardly needed my involvement."

"Dealing with the police, you mean."

"No," I said. "Well, yeah. Except it all started before they came. With the hog that was supposed to be pastrami."

"So a roast hog made you feel irrelevant?"

"Not the hog per se. But the screwup drove home how much I don't know about running a delicatessen. It *should* have been a pastrami. It really should have."

"Right, I think you've established that—"

"My uncle did the deli's ordering himself, Caz," I interrupted. "He wrote all his suppliers' names in notebooks, but now they're scattered everywhere . . . and even Thomasina's clueless about where he bought half his stuff." A sigh escaped me. "Bottom line, I called a meat wholesaler in Joelton for a pastrami and instead got Porky the Pig after a serious forest fire. I'm not prepared to fill Murray's shoes—or cowboy boots as the case may be."

Cazzie looked thoughtful. "You handled the situation, didn't you?"

"No," I said. "All I did was spend a fortune on crisis management. And look how things turned out."

"Gwen, give yourself credit. You're drawing a connection between two things that couldn't be more separate. What happened to Buster had nothing to do with that pig."

I shook my head. "I'm telling you, the pig was a honey-glazed bad omen. And I've got a hunch more trouble's on the way."

"Like what?"

"I wish I could put a finger on it," I said with a shrug. "When the police detective arrived and took charge of the scene, I sensed some kind of tension between him and Thom. He seemed pleasant enough at first, but his attitude got downright nasty after they exchanged words."

"Did you try asking Thomasina what it was about?"

"No," I said. "And I got the distinct impression she didn't think it was any of my business."

Cazzie quietly reached for her coffee and sipped.

I did the same, but only after eating a mouthful of Cocoa Puffs from my cereal bowl. I was thinking maybe I should've had the Lucky Charms instead. I needed a drastic reversal of fortune. A green shamrock marshmallow surely couldn't have hurt my chances.

"There's something more to this," Cazzie said. "Isn't there?"

I nodded slowly. "I don't understand why the cops put us in lockdown last night," I said. "McClintock—"

"That's the meanie detective?"

"Right, sorry," I said. "He not only orders his men to bag samples of our food, but has them seize our order pads and kitchen tickets."

Cazzie's eyes had narrowed. She was a junior partner with a law office, and though her expertise lay in intellectual property and copyrights, it was clear the attorney in her was paying attention.

"Did he tell you why they took all that stuff?"

"And actually *not* keep me in the dark for a change?" I said, and expelled another sigh. "Caz, you couldn't have pried an explanation out of him with a crowbar. I only got one because—"

I was interrupted by the sound of clunky little feet thumping up behind me. Snapping my head toward the kitchen entry, I saw Cazzie's youngest appear there in a T-shirt and over-the-knee cargo shorts. A toothbrush poked from one corner of his foam-slathered mouth.

"Jimmy, what are you *doing*?" Cazzie asked.

*"Cl kpshgng thsnk!"* Jimmy said.

Cazzie shot him a disapproving look. "Care to repeat that so I can understand you?"

He pulled the brush out of his mouth. "Cole won't stop hogging the sink," he said. "He—"

"Not true! I didn't do anything wrong."

In case you're wondering, that adamant denial had come from none other than Cole himself, who was in the bathroom down the hall.

"Did so!" Toothpaste bubbled from Jimmy's lips. "He wouldn't get off the stool or stop smiling at his ugly puss in the mirror!"

"I wasn't smiling," Cole shouted. "I was checking for *food crud*—"

"Then finish checking and let your brother rinse his mouth," Cazzie said. She glanced up at her wall clock, a green apple design she'd made in her ceramics workshop, don't ask where she finds the time. "Aunt Grace said she'd be here in ten minutes, so you'd better have your beach bags ready."

Cole spun his head around toward the entry. "See, I told you to get away from—"

"Go rinse!" Cazzie ordered. "This instant!"

Jimmy frowned, turned on his sneaker bottoms, and dashed from the room.

"Motherhood . . . such a pleasure," Cazzie said with a small headshake. "Thank heavens for relatives that give me sanity breaks once in a while."

I smiled. Grace, her sister-in-law, had two kids of her own and was taking the gathered bunch on an overnight outing to Nashville Shores.

"Chris is away on a long one, huh?"

"He's back on an international track . . . Memphis, Chicago, London," Cazzie said. "It's a week-long trip sequence. Eight days to be precise. They've got him doing two a month, plus a domestic run." She paused. "How'd you know?"

I shrugged. Her husband was a commercial airline pilot, and he'd been on a domestic routine when we first met. But the airline had done some reshuffling because of employee cutbacks.

"I don't need to be psychic," I said. "The boys always act up when their dad's gone for long stretches."

Cazzie raised her cup, took a sip of coffee. "His new schedule's hard on them."

I nodded.

"Hard on me too," she said.

I nodded again.

Caz sighed. "Whiny, whiny," she said. "I shouldn't complain."

I noticed that she looked a bit awkward. Cazzie knew about my ex, Phil, and his personal strip club revue. But I wasn't that sensitive. Being divorced was lonely. But no lonelier than living with a man whose extramarital affairs would have left Tiger Woods holding his putter in exhaustion.

"You never finished telling me about last night," she said, changing the subject.

I tried to recall where I'd left off.

"The food samples," Caz prompted. "You mentioned that you eventually learned why the police took them."

"Oh, right." I ate some cereal. "Except it wasn't me who found out. It was my waitress, A.J. I think you've met her."

Cazzie nodded. "That pretty blonde who gets all the looks."

"*Looks* aren't the half of it, but let's not go there right now," I said meaningfully. "Anyway, one of the cops spilled the beans to A.J. when he took her statement. He mentioned a case in Lexington, Kentucky. This was just last month . . . a restaurant customer died from the food. The poor guy ordered the Harvest Chicken, which I guess is a chicken, herb and vegetable platter. But somebody messed up and he got the Caribbean Reef Chicken by mistake."

"The dish tasted so bad it killed him?"

"Very funny, Caz. The fact is there was crabmeat in that Caribbean Reef dish. He was allergic to seafood and had a severe reaction."

"That's *terrible*."

"I'll say. It gave him fatal convulsions on the spot."

"But it sounds to me like a freak accident," Cazzie said, shaking her head. "What's it got to do with you?"

"Nothing whatsoever," I said. "Lexington's a long way from here. And Sergeant didn't convulse at all. I hate to sound cold about it, but he just dropped dead. Turned purple and, boom, hit the floor. Well, the floor of the *stage*."

Cazzie looked thoughtful. She topped off her coffee, motioned toward my empty cup with her carafe. I shook my head, having already reached my two-cup limit for the morning. But I was admittedly ogling the cereal boxes again.

"You said this incident in Kentucky took place a month ago?" she asked.

"Right."

"Then it's possible the police here are only being extra cautious," she said. "Did you ask if they noticed any parallels between the two deaths? Other than both taking place in restaurants?"

"How could I? I didn't know a thing about the man in Lexington till A.J. gave me the scoop . . . and that was after the cops left." I sighed. "Think about it a second. This is something a police officer confided to my employee while I was practically hanging out on the sidelines. I'd might as well not have been there. I was useless, not to mention helpless. A—"

"—gefilte fish out of water."

"You've got it," I said, dotting the sentence in the air with my fingertip.

We sat quietly in the warm June sunshine. With the Great Toothpaste Spitting War suspended by maternal decree, we could hear the boys hurrying around their room as they prepared to be picked up.

"From a legal perspective, you face a couple of potential issues," Cazzie said, shifting into lawyer mode. "One is your restaurant's potential responsibility . . ."

"Huh?" My eyes widened. "Wait a minute, Caz. Wasn't it you who called Buster Sergeant's death a freak accident!"

"That's why I used the word *potential*," she said. "I'm almost sure you won't have any problems. But it wouldn't hurt for me to speak with a colleague of mine who's a liability attorney."

"And spread the word that Murray's Deli does toxic catering?"

Cazzie offered a thin smile. "Don't worry. I'll make sure everything's discussed under privilege—"

"Okay, let's change the subject before I hyper-ventilate," I said, glancing out the window. "It's a beautiful morning. I wonder how it'll be the rest of the day? I *love* beautiful days. Have you heard the weather forecast, Caz?"

Caz sat there as her green apple clock ticked away into the silence. "Gwen, trust me, you just need to settle in a little," she said. "I'm a South Side girl. Never thought I'd be happy living outside Chicago. Then I meet Chris in an O'Hare waiting lounge . . . and zap! We're engaged before I know what's hit me. Cut ahead a year, I'm in Nashville, married to him, listening to his favorite hometown country music stations on the radio. And these days . . . well, you *know* how much I like singing along when I drive the kids to baseball and soccer practice."

"So you're saying precisely what? That I should get preggers and become a soccer mom who's memorized Tammy Wynette lyrics?"

Cazzie shooed me with a wave of her hand.

"Moving here was a big change for me," she said. "It took a while to make the adjustment. I don't know about feeling like a gefilte fish. But I was definitely an Aurelio's pizza in a Domino's box."

I looked at her. "I'm not sure the comparison works."

"Want an alternate?"

"Maybe next time."

Cazzie smiled gently. I smiled back.

"I'm not claiming my experiences were identical to yours . . . but I can relate to enough of them," she said after a bit. "Give Nashville a chance. I think you'll fall in love with it, same as I did . . . and I *do* love this place. The weather, the people, everything about it. That includes those Goo Goo bars I gave you, and am wondering if you've sampled yet."

I didn't answer, afraid to hurt Caz's feelings. How could I own up to passing on the Goo Goos so soon after she'd gone gaga over Nashville?

Fortunately I was saved by her sister-in-law. Well, the sound of her car pulling up to the sidewalk out front.

As Caz craned her head to look out the window, the boys stampeded into the kitchen with their beach totes, playfully flopped up my already mutinous mop of hair (I'm a lifer in the Unruly Hair Club for Jews), and took turns hurrying to get their sports bottles out of the fridge.

It gave me the perfect opening to exit gracefully before Cazzie could ask about the Goo Goo bars again.

"You leaving?" she said as I pushed up off my chair. "Grace is popping in for a minute—"

"I'll catch her on my way out," I said. "It's getting late, and I have lots to do at the deli."

She looked at the clock. "It's seven in the

morning. You don't usually head over there for another hour."

I halted with my fingers around the doorknob, glanced over at her.

"One thing's for sure, Caz . . . this isn't my usual day," I said, telling the absolute truth.

# Chapter Four

Around eight o'clock that morning, I was at the deli heading downstairs from my office, the Passover photo of Uncle Murray and me tucked under my arm, a hammer and box of nails in my hand. I'd found the hammer in the top drawer of my desk and the nails in its paper clip organizer.

I was sure Murray could have found a better place to keep them, but you didn't see many bare-chested Jewish Mr. Fixits with low-slung tool belts around their hips. Of course, Jewish country-and-western performers were even less common sights, and my uncle had shown plenty of chutzpah and determination bucking that particular stereotype.

Meanwhile, I guess that I still had Lucky Charms on my brain, because I'd removed the picture from the wall thinking I needed *some* kind charm to reverse my karma. I had a new location in mind that seemed just right. It would be far more potent—and appropriate—there than a green marshmallow shamrock.

Though I'd entered the building through the side entrance, and hadn't yet stepped into the dining room, I had known Newt and his kitchen staffers were hard at work . . . and would have been long before my arrival, since they always came in early to prepare for lunch. Not even the tin ceiling under my floorboards could keep the aromas of knishes baking in the oven, chicken matzo ball soup on the range, and especially our traditional Saturday cholent from wafting up to my office.

For a while, I had sat there just sniffing and savoring the delicious smells. A house specialty, the cholent was a Jewish version of poor boy stew developed in fifteenth-century Eastern Europe using readily available ingredients—beans, barley, potatoes, onions and beef, simmered with garlic, paprika, and other seasonings. As Murray had told me once upon a time, observant Jews were prohibited from lighting cooking fires on the Sabbath under religious law, so they'd gotten imaginative and developed a warm winter meal they could start before sundown on Sabbath Eve and let stand overnight on a low flame.

The secret of Murray's cholent was a secret combination of added herbs and a unique cooking method that went back hundreds of years to the dish's peasant beginnings. Far as I knew, he'd shared the full recipe and process with only two people—Newt and me. That meant not even Thomasina was privy to it.

Right now, its scent had imparted a sense of inner calm that I hadn't felt since my plunge into Kosher Karaoke night hell . . . or possibly since the coming of its wicked messenger, Crispy the Pig. It had also stirred my appetite despite the expanded clumps of Cocoa Puffs in my tireless tummy. As the originator and sole devotee of the Gwen Silver Smoker's Diet, I knew the cigarette I'd had while driving in would have accelerated my metabolism—and thus my caloric burn rate—enough to allow for a forkful or two of the cholent, and perhaps a wee sampling of chicken soup. It would be a personal act of defiance, refuting the whispers of possible food contamination A.J. had heard from Lover Cop. And hey, if I could make stuffing my face a matter of principle, why not? Was there ever a better cause for rationalization?

But first things first. I had wanted that picture from my office hung in its perfect new spot.

I was about to push through the double doors into the restaurant when I heard someone singing along to the accompaniment of an acoustic guitar. After a split second, I recognized Luke's voice.

This I *hadn't* expected. My lunch servers wouldn't arrive for at least another hour, and Luke had been scheduled for the dinner shift. Also, we didn't offer entertainment with our food, karaoke night being the lone, currently lamentable, exception. Luke's singing and guitar strumming, if not his stonewashed denim butt-huggers, were reserved for club gigs and auditions. All of which were gyrated—ah, I mean, performed—on his own time.

I opened the door partway and stood listening to him.

*A self-made man wearin' bootheels of*
*    leather,*

*Come up from nowhere on roads windin'*
*an' weathered.*
*Died too young, but stayed true to his song,*
*Till he dropped down dead 'fore anyone*
*knew what was wrong.*

*Now I'm standin' outside his big truck 'n*
*auto lot,*
*A wonderin' how many more tomorrows*
*it got.*
*There's a lonesome Dodge pickup with a*
*dusty tag in the window,*
*A slick Toyota hybrid sittin' in limbo.*

*Buyers and sellers, I watch 'em all grieve,*
*Then after a while, see them turn round*
*an' leave.*
*It's hit 'em where it hurts, hit 'em hard*
*one by one:*
*Without good ol' Sarge givin' orders, ain't*
*no sales gettin' done.*

*Lord, my heart's a V8 engine, and its*
*cylinders are achin',*
*There's an emptiness inside like a parkin'*
*spot vacant.*
*All them rubber tires gone still, them quiet*
*chassis of steel,*
*How're they gonna get sold without*
*Buster's fair an' honest deals?*

"Enough!" I pushed open the doors from the
kitchen and saw Luke sitting on a chair near one of

the tables, the guitar across his lap. "What's that song you're playing?"

As he glanced up from his fret board, I realized the kid was in the same clothes he'd worn the night before. And that he hadn't shaved or combed his hair.

"'Morning, Nash," he said. "I'm almost done with a new ballad. Figure I might call it 'Salute to the Sarge.' Or somethin' simple like "Good-bye Buster.' You care to hear the rest?"

"No."

Luke just stared at me. He seemed totally blind to my look of prune-faced annoyance. Maybe it was the eyelid lifter and super concealer.

"I sure could use your opinion. They're holdin' open calls for *Nashville's Hottest,* that new singer-songwriter contest they got on television. I figured the tune would show my sensitive side so people can see I ain't just a shakin' hunk of beefcake. And bein' *topical,* it could give me an edge over the competition—"

"Don't you dare even consider it, Luke."

"You thinkin' the song's no good?"

"Never mind," I said. "What're you doing here at this hour anyway?"

"Stuck around until the police finished their work and I could lock up," Luke said. "By then it was past two in the morning. I felt too pooped to drive home and decided I'd crash here."

I abruptly regretted my snippiness. It had occurred to me that Luke probably hadn't spoken to A.J. since last night, and had no idea why the cops had taken their food samples. He wasn't dumb. Immature, yep. Prone to recurrent bouts of self-absorption and madly in love with his mirror, check. But I didn't know anybody who was quicker to do me a favor . . . and his staying behind to close the place had been a huge one.

"I don't think cylinders really ache," I said contritely. "And the line about your heart being an engine with an empty parking spot's a mixed metaphor."

"A *what*?"

"I'll explain later. Meanwhile, follow me . . . I need a little assist."

I led the way up front and around the counter. On the wall behind the cash register—mounted slightly to one side—was a collection of rave newspaper and magazine reviews of the deli, a clear acrylic block showcasing the first bill that Uncle Murray took in, our liquor license, and the obligatory health department notices on the Heimlich maneuver and drinking alcoholic beverages during pregnancy. I looked at the diagram and momentarily imagined Buster Sergeant's face superimposed on the figure of the choking victim in the Heimlich diagram. Then I frowned and shifted my attention to a collage of photos showing Murray with the dozens of legendary country and rockabilly performers who'd been his pals and regular diners: Conway Twitty, Ronnie Milsap, The Blue Moon Boys, Buck Owens, Wanda Jackson (he'd had a crush on her all his life, and was really beaming in that shot), Roy Orbison, Johnny Cash, Dolly

Parton . . . it seemed he'd known and fed every superstar who'd ever walked along Music Row.

I stood facing the register, my eyes on a bare section of wall directly above it. Whether by fate, coincidence, or some combination of the two, that space had been there the very first time I entered the deli.

It was perfect, all right. Perfection *defined.*

"The picture goes here." I stretched to hold the frame up where I wanted it. "Right here."

Luke studied the photo. "That's you with Murray, ain't it?" he asked.

"Yeah."

"It's great. I seen it in the office. He must've had it up there forever."

"Yeah."

"Want me to put it on the wall? I'm taller'n you."

No kidding. So was Ms. Pac-Man. I kept the thought to myself and shook my head no. "You go back in the aisle and make sure I hang it straight—"

The telephone next to the cash register rang. *Early for customers,* I thought. Still holding up the photo with both hands, I glanced over my shoulder as Luke answered.

"Murray's Deli," he said. "Yeah, right. Hang on. I'll see if she's in." He covered the mouthpiece, gave me a guarded look. "It's a lawyer, Nash."

Uh-oh. I'd flashed back on Cazzie's advice about liability protection.

"He or she give you a name?" I whispered.

*"He,"* Luke said with a nod. "It's Liar-somethin'."

We exchanged glances, and he nodded to indicate

he hadn't made that up. I carefully set the picture frame down on the counter and took the receiver from him.

"Yes?" I said.

"Good morning, Ms. Silver," a voice said in my ear. "You *are* Gwendolyn Silver, correct?"

"That's right."

"Wonderful. I'm Cyrus Liarson. My law firm represents—"

"What was your second name again?"

"Liarson . . . an unfortunate familial legacy for someone in my profession." He gave a rote-sounding chuckle. "I once considered shortening it, but that simply would have left me a 'Liar.'"

I caught the pun but didn't say anything.

"All humor aside, Ms. Silver, I represent—"

*Buster Sergeant,* I thought with a catch in my breath.

"Ramsey Holdings," he said.

"Ramsey *who*?"

"Not who, what," Liarson said. "It is the most prominent real-estate firm in central Tennessee . . . surely you are familiar with the name."

Actually, I wasn't. Nor was I impressed by Liarson's mention of it, as his tone suggested I ought to be. I did, however, feel like sighing with relief. Whatever he wanted, it presumably wasn't connected to Buster Sergeant's death.

"I'm pleased to have you on the phone at long last," he went on. "Having tried to reach you for weeks—"

"Reach me how?"

"Well, I left several messages—"

"Mr. Liarson, I don't mean to keep interrupting. But I haven't gotten any messages from you."

"You haven't?"

"No, sorry."

"Hmm. That's odd." He paused. "I must have called three or four times."

I raised an eyebrow. "Do you remember with whom you spoke?"

"Yes. In fact, I made definite note of it. . . give me one second while I check my calendar notes." I heard him tap away at a computer keyboard. "Here we are . . . it was your manager. Thomasina Jackson, is that correct?"

"Yes . . ."

"Then there's been no confusion on my part," Liarson said. "I'd assumed you were tied up with your reopening and unable to return my calls."

I noticed a questioning look on Luke's face as I reached into my purse for a cigarette. He seemed curious about what had gotten me so aggravated. Not more curious than I was about Thomasina, though. She hadn't uttered a peep about those calls.

"In any event," Liarson said into the silence, "I've been eager to have a conversation with you. On behalf of Mr. Ramsey."

"*Mister?* I thought you just told me you're the attorney for—"

"Ramsey Holdings is the name of a corporation whose president and major shareholder is Royce Ramsey," Liarson said. "Technically I manage his personal affairs. But I will on occasion handle his more important commercial ventures."

My eyebrow shot higher up my forehead. Granted,

I was overtired, irritable, and admittedly ready to pounce. But Liarson's pushiness had been getting on my nerves . . . and finding out Thom was keeping secrets bugged me to no end.

"Look," I said, "I'm busy, so can you get to the point?"

"Absolutely," Liarson said. "I would like to make arrangements between you and my client—"

"What for?"

"A meeting."

"About?"

"Mr. Ramsey would rather tell you in person."

"And I'd rather hear it from *you* over the phone."

A pause. Liarson cleared his throat. "Yes, certainly," he said. "I read about the incident at your restaurant in today's paper. Our community has suffered a profound loss. But as an attorney, I've seen opportunity arise from the worst of tragedies. It turns out Mr. Ramsey has prepared a generous offer for your property at *precisely* the right moment to divest yourself of a financial albatross—"

"What are you talking about?" I asked, the cigarette hanging from my mouth. "Are you saying your boss wants to buy my *deli*?"

"He isn't my boss, Ms. Silver . . . our relationship is that of an attorney and client," Liarson said, betraying the faintest hint of peevishness. "Also, I'd make a distinction between the restaurant and its location. It's the second that primarily interests Mr. Ramsey despite its low market value."

"Hang on. You're joking, right? We're in the *busiest* part of town."

"In a passé sense, perhaps—"

"Passé, *schmassé,*" I said. "The convention center's practically across the street. Bridgestone Arena's right over on Fourth—"

"Yes, yes. And in a sense that's my point."

"How so?"

"My client is best suited to explain, which is why he would prefer meeting with you face-to-face," Liarson said. "In the meantime, suffice it to say trends change . . . even downtown. Mr. Ramsey has built his reputation on foresight, vision, and maximizing his acquired assets. He has the resources to absorb current and near-future losses and look toward eventual redevelopment. Your neighbors came to understand this to their considerable gain."

That raised my curiosity. It also raised my eyebrow some more. In fact, I was thinking that if it got any higher, it would probably reach the top of my head and start down the other side.

"What neighbors?" I said, taking his bait.

"It isn't my place to say, but as a newcomer to the Metro area you might want to make some inquiries," Liarson replied in a cryptic tone. "Ms. Silver, kosher dining has never been the vogue in Nashville. But my employer respects your restaurant's longevity . . . its niche popularity. As a generous quid pro quo, therefore, he has made it plain he's willing to consider a singular, mutually attractive arrangement."

I frowned. "Actually he hasn't made *anything* plain, since we've never even spoken—"

"And again, he would like to remedy that as

soon as possible," Liarson said. "You may find this offer comes at an opportune juncture."

"You're repeating yourself—"

"Last night's incident aside, I mean," Liarson said. "Our market surveys indicate Murray's Delicatessen was an owner-driven establishment. Which is to say your uncle's personality gave it a unique stamp of appeal—and drew its clientele. Upon his death, it instantly became a fading landmark."

That made me bristle. "Last time I looked, your *boss* wasn't privy to my cash receipts."

"Ms. Silver, if you would please listen to me—"

"Forget it." I'd nestled the receiver between my chin and shoulder and was waving my Pall Mall around in the air. "I think your attitude's condescending and insulting . . ."

"Ms. Silver—"

I heard a beep in my ear, glanced at the telephone, and noticed a second button light up on the console. A call was coming in on another line.

Enough was enough. Disconnecting Liarson with a jab of my finger, I pushed the flashing button. "Murray's."

"Ms. Silver?"

Déjà vu. Or maybe not so much. I'd recognized the voice and it didn't resemble the attorney's a bit. "Detective McClintock?"

"Yes," he said. "I'm glad I caught you."

"Oh?"

"I wasn't certain what time you'd be at the restaurant. We need to talk."

I shoved the Pall Mall back in my mouth. His tone bothered me. It sounded . . . I don't know.

*Loaded.* But plucky native New Yorker that I was, my first instinct was to tackle whatever he had to say head-on—

Okay, I'm lying. Maybe it's the post-traumatic stress of seeing my fraud of an ex-hub led out of our apartment in handcuffs, but dealing with the cops always makes me want to dive into a rabbit hole.

"I'm a million kinds of busy right now," I said, figuring the same remark, more or less, had worked to put Liarson in a defensive position. "How about you call back this afternoon—?"

"I need you at the station, Ms. Silver."

My heart knocked. "When?"

"The sooner, the better. As I said, there are things we need to discuss."

I took a deep, long breath and almost sucked my cigarette down my windpipe. "What sort of things?"

McClintock didn't answer. I hung on, waiting.

"Look, I'll give you a heads-up, although I probably shouldn't," he finally said in a low voice. "Keep this in your pocket all right?"

*Knock-knock-knock.* "All right," I said.

"The medical examiner's turned in a preliminary lab workup," McClintock said. "They don't usually come this fast. But Buster Sergeant's a VIP, and that tends to speed along the process." His voice dropped another notch. "I'm the first to see the report and it isn't good."

I scanned the floor for that hole I felt like bolting into. No go. "What's it say?"

"It indicates Sergeant was deliberately poisoned at your restaurant," McClintock said.

"Poi—*how?*"

"Ms. Silver, we can discuss it when you get here. I'm right up the street. The precinct's right in the tower at Bridgestone. Take the elevator to the third floor—"

"I know where to find it," I said. "Give me fifteen minutes."

McClintock grunted. "I'll be in my office," he said.

# Chapter Five

"How's it now?" I glanced over at Luke from behind the counter. "Still crooked?"

"Push it thataways," he said, motioning slightly to the left.

I made the adjustment to the picture frame, looked at him again. His face screwing up with concentration, Luke tilted his hand leftward by added degrees.

"A little more, little more . . . there you go," he said.

I came around into the aisle, gave the photograph of Murray and me an approving look. Before rushing off to see McClintock, I'd decided to finish what I had started at the deli.

"My lucky charm," I said, thinking it had better radiate some positive vibes but *fast*.

Luke nodded appreciatively. "It fits, Nash. I mean, like, I kinda feel this is where it's always belonged," he said, his eyes on the photo. "You an' Murray together straight outta the Wayback machine."

I gave him a sidewise glance. "Rocky and Bullwinkle?"

"Got all their cartoons on DVD."

I was impressed. I also knew I'd stood there admiring the picture as long as I could.

"I'd better get a move on," I said.

"Where you goin'?"

It was a good question. Unfortunately, McClintock had asked me to stay mum. "Out . . . I have to head out for a while," I replied. Slick, huh?

Luke gave me a look. "But you just *got* here."

"I'll explain later," I said. "You hold the fort in the meantime."

"This is about whoever was on the phone that second time," Luke said. "Ain't it, Nash?"

I didn't answer. Considering how obnoxious McClintock had been the night before, I couldn't figure out why he'd tipped me off to the coroner's report. But whatever his reasons, I appreciated it.

Luke was staring at me in silence, open concern on his face now.

I smiled faintly, squeezed his elbow.

"Later," I repeated.

Grabbing my purse from the counter, I hurried out the door and walked east toward Bridgestone, which looks like the flying saucer from *The Day the Earth Stood Still* parked smack atop a Broadway office building. Metro Police Central's entrance was set back under the saucer's jutting outer rim, and came up right before you reached the Nashville visitor information tower at the corner of Fifth Avenue.

I turned in, rode the elevator to the third floor,

then gave my name to an officer at the precinct desk and told him Detective McClintock was expecting me. He'd no sooner pushed his intercom button than McClintock appeared through a doorway.

"Ms. Silver." He glanced at his wristwatch. "Right on time."

He was smiling politely, but I still hadn't forgotten his brusque manner when we were introduced.

"Always," I said with a neutral shrug.

His eyes briefly met mine. Then he pushed the door open wider with his arm, stepped aside, and gestured toward the hall beyond. "My office is the third on your right."

I went into the corridor. One, two, three. We stopped in front of McClintock's office, and he held the door again and followed me through, motioning to a chair in front of his desk.

I sat. Though the room was probably about the same size as my own office over the deli, it gave the appearance of being much larger absent all the carnage Murray had left behind. In fact it was uncluttered and sparsely furnished—there was the desk, a metal credenza, a file cabinet, and nothing else. The desktop was clear except for a computer screen and keyboard, matching wooden pen and paper-clip holders, and an autographed baseball in a round plastic trophy case.

I should also point out the single manila file folder that seemed to be waving howdy-doo from the middle of the blotter.

As McClintock sat down opposite me, I stopped staring at the folder long enough to notice an obligatory police tackboard on the wall. That and the framed photo of a baseball team to his immediate right. A younger version of him was crouched in the front row of players. Their orange-gold uniform shirts had bold white Ts on the left breast. Keen guesser that I was, I figured it for a high school or college varsity team.

McClintock regarded me a moment, his fingertips on the edge of the desk. "I want to thank you for coming on short notice, Ms. Silver—"

"You're welcome," I said. "And Gwen would be fine."

He nodded. "About last night, Gwen . . . I'd like to ask you a few questions."

The desire was mutual. "Is that the folder?" I said, dipping my chin at it.

McClintock gave me a questioning glance.

"I assume that's the lab report on Buster Sergeant," I said. "The one you mentioned when you called."

He nodded. "The initial tox findings, yes."

"Tox as in . . ."

"Toxicology, sorry," McClintock said. "We'll get to it, I promise. But first we should talk."

I considered reminding him that he hadn't made any such stipulation over the phone, but decided against it. I had nothing to hide.

"Sure," I said. "What can I do to help?"

"For openers, can you tell me how a serving of food goes from the kitchen to the table for a catered event."

I shrugged. "It all depends."

"On . . . ?"

"Different things. Is it an appetizer, main course, or dessert? Do you mean a beef dish? Poultry? Latkes?" I paused. The latter weren't exactly a Southern staple. "Those are—"

"Potato pancakes, I know," McClintock said. "Let's stick to a main dinner course for now. Roast beef hypothetically. Be as specific as you can."

I looked at him. He didn't sound like he was being too hypothetical.

"Well, the first step's actually when the roast beef's ordered. For an event the available dishes are set ahead of time. There's an online ordering process so whoever's throwing the affair can choose what courses are served for dinner, give us the number of guests, and then pay or leave a deposit electronically when the event's booked."

"Sounds like a pretty modern system."

"I think it's two or three years old," I said. "My uncle was anything *but* modern. But he hated catered parties."

"Why's that?"

"He felt they were unprofitable. I don't know why. It *does* get a little complicated when guests start asking for extras. Some restaurants have a firm policy of sticking to the preordered course list."

"And Murray's?"

"If we can whip a dish together, and the booker's okay with it, we'll try to make the diner happy," I said. "Anyway, my uncle's accountant came up with the computerized system when the deli's website was designed."

"That's Artemis Duff."

I looked at McClintock. "Yeah . . . do you know Artie?"

"I think we may have met." He drummed his fingers on the manila folder. "Okay, I think I'm clear on the ordering procedure. Getting back to the night of the event, and our roast beef . . ."

"Right," I said. "Once it leaves the oven, our head cook sets it on a platter—"

"That's Mr. Trout."

"Newt, yes," I said. "He'll carve the roast according to how many orders he's gotten, put each slice on a plate, and spoon or drizzle some of the cooking juices onto them."

"So they stay moist."

"Right."

"And then?"

"Our waiters garnish the dishes."

"With parsley, that sort of thing?"

"Could be parsley, a carrot flower, a pineapple wedge . . . again, it's determined by the meal. Newt has his staff prep his garnishes ahead of time. His sides too."

"And the side orders are also added by your waiters."

"Yes, exactly."

McClintock nodded. "Okay, what's next?"

"That's about it. Guests at an affair have a choice of three or four main courses. Since this usually means there'll be multiple portions of the same dish at a table, our servers will bring them out to their stations together on delivery carts."

"And then serve them off the carts, yes?"

"Exactly."

McClintock thoughtfully drummed his fingers against the desktop.

"One or two more questions," he said. "If I remember correctly, when a waiter writes an order in his pad, he gives a carbon copy to the kitchen staff. Hangs it on a rail . . . that's the kitchen ticket, right?"

"Right," I said. "Nowadays, most places have gone over to electronic systems. Rather than turn in a handwritten ticket, the waiter keys the order into a computerized cash register. Then it either shoots out of a printer or appears on a display screen in the kitchen. It's considered more efficient because nobody has to decipher a waiter's scribbled handwriting. But we still do it the old-fashioned way at the deli."

"Any particular reason?"

"Impractical as it might be, I want things to stay the same as when my late uncle ran it. Whenever possible, that is. The only change I've made is having our waiters turn in the originals."

"Instead of the carbons."

I nodded. "If you don't press down hard enough with your pen, the writing can be light and illegible even for someone with decent penmanship. It eliminates that problem."

"And the copy . . . ?"

"Ordinarily becomes the guest check. It's different with catered affairs, since the host almost always covers the entire tab."

"In which case, there wouldn't be any guest checks."

"That's right."

"Since everything's paid for in advance."

"Right."

"Online, yes?"

"Again, that would depend. Our minimum deposit is fifty percent. So the host can pay the full amount online when the event's booked, or make a partial payment. The rest is due by the day of the event and can be made in person," I said. "As far as the checks, we toss the carbons and keep the originals for our records—and for whoever booked the affair in case they want Xeroxes for their own bookkeeping."

The detective was drumming his fingers again. "Can everyone in the kitchen see the tickets? Say, for instance, a dishwasher?"

"I suppose. But I don't know who'd bother reading them besides the cooks. And the waiters when they make their pickups."

"How about access to the kitchen? Am I right that any member of your staff can go in and out?"

"Why not? It doesn't exactly hold classified nuclear secrets."

McClintock gave me a blunt look. "Good of you to share that information," he said.

I instantly regretted my little snipe. While you could argue he'd earned it the night before, I had to admit he was making nice . . . well, very *nicely*.

"Sorry," I said. "I didn't get much sleep and it's left me kind of ragged this morning."

McClintock studied my face. He'd stopped his finger tapping for the moment.

"I understand," he said. Then hesitated. "You don't look it, by the way."

"Hmm?"

"Ragged."

"Oh." Was that a compliment I'd heard? *My over-and-under eye makeup at work.*

McClintock was still watching my face. "As for what you said about only cooks and waiters reading the kitchen tickets . . ."

"I meant that when you work in a restaurant, you're really just concerned with your own job," I said. "The kitchen's a busy place. Nothing gets done unless everybody sticks to whatever they're supposed to be doing."

He sat looking thoughtful, his fingertips poised to rap the desk again. But he surprised me by instead reaching for his file folder and opening it.

"I can't share too many details about the autopsy results," he said, eyeing the thin sheaf of documents in the folder. "But I can clear up some things you might've wondered while tossing and turning last night."

I nodded into the pause. And waited.

"The good news is that it wasn't the restaurant's fault in any sense that would leave it legally responsible," he said. "The coroner found nothing to indicate bacterial food contamination, mercury from the pipes, anaphylactic shock . . . I don't know if you heard about it, but there was a case resulting from a mix-up in Kentucky a little while ago."

"That rings a vague little bell," I lied, careful not to out A.J.'s horny mole with the Metro police. I wouldn't have wanted to make trouble for him—or lose our inside source.

McClintock fell into another silence, lowering his eyes to the folder as he flipped through its contents. Then he looked back at my face. And held the look.

"Is this the bad news part?" I asked.

"I'm afraid so," he said. "Gwen, it's the coroner's firm opinion that Buster Sergeant was murdered."

I stared at him in disbelief. "I don't . . . that is, it can't be . . ."

"Have you ever heard of carbofuran?"

I shook my head.

"How about something called Furadan?"

"No."

"They're different names for the same toxic compound," McClintock said. "For a while, ranchers used it to kill coyotes that preyed on their cattle. That's been prohibited for over a decade . . . but much as I hate to admit it, some local environmental authorities still put on blinders for their friends and constituents."

I considered that a second. "I'm guessing the prohibition didn't come about because of some outpouring of sympathy for coyotes. Not that using it sounds very humane."

McClintock shrugged. "It isn't," he said. "But the larger problem with carbofuran is that it can also do away with innocent wildlife, including endangered species. One Missouri man, an agricultural farmer, got charged with killing three bald eagles and using poisoned bait in violation of federal regulations. Also killed a red-tailed hawk, a great horned owl, a bunch of other protected animals. I seem to remember President Bubba pardoning him before he left office."

I was staring at him again. "Was just *any* fool allowed to buy the stuff?"

"Before I answer that, I'd have to know where the fool lived and what he wanted it for," McClintock said with a thin smile. "I poked around the Internet and read about a Kenyan cattleman who wiped out a whole pride of lions with less than you'd use to fill an eyedropper. That wasn't an isolated occurrence either . . . it got so bad there the whole species almost became extinct. Now it's illegal to pick it up over the counter in Kenya, but legal in neighboring countries—and I'll let you guess how thorough they are at border interdiction."

"A bribe for every open hand, huh?"

"That pretty much describes things," McClintock said. "In America, the EPA threatened to throw a blanket ban on carbofuran till the manufacturer decided to limit its sale to farmers who grow certain types of crops. They use it as an insecticide for resistant pests and feed it to their plants through the soil."

I sat there absorbing that. Porous borders in Kenya, legal loopholes and cronyism in the U.S. of A. It sounded as if the chemical could be gotten very easily if you wanted it enough.

"The level of carbofuran found in Buster's system would've taken out ten men," McClintock went on. "There was enough in his food to kill at least another ten."

"You mean in our *brisket*?"

McClintock nodded. "Everybody who ordered the beef at your deli was given three slices . . . does that seem accurate?"

I struggled to pry my tongue from the roof of my mouth. "Right. Three per portion. That's how Newt serves it . . ."

McClintock nodded again. "The undigested meat in Buster's stomach was poisoned. Also whatever was left on his plate. And he'd eaten almost two slices before he got up to sing."

"But that was only a little while after we sent out the orders."

McClintock nodded a third time. "He wolfed his food down fast, and the toxin took him down even faster," he said. "Gives you an idea of its potency."

I sat looking stunned and astonished. "I don't understand . . . how could it have gotten into Buster's portion?"

"Our best guess is it was injected after the brisket was put on his plate."

"Inj—you mean with a *needle*?"

"That makes the most sense. A syringe is efficient. You know the chemical's going where you want it. And its exact concentration. Besides, the other portions at his table tested clean."

"What about the uncut beef in the kitchen?"

"Clean too"

"So you think . . . what? That somebody at my restaurant had it *in* for Buster?"

McClintock was quiet. He shut the file folder and pushed it to the middle of his desk.

"It depends whether the person who dosed the food knew which plate Buster was getting," he said. "All that's definite is somebody wanted to kill somebody else."

I resisted the urge to yell "Cut!" while making a chopping gesture with my hand. "Detective . . . I'm telling you right now that there are no homicidal maniacs working for me."

"I didn't say that."

"You didn't have to," I said. "It isn't like a customer can tiptoe into the kitchen without being noticed. And the food couldn't have been tampered with in the dining room."

"You're positive?"

"One hundred percent," I said. The real figure was probably somewhere between forty and sixty percent—or maybe thirty and forty—but I admit to having been in profound denial. "Buster's table was full of guests. He was surrounded by people. I can't believe they all could've missed seeing someone shoot his food full of poison with a hypodermic like . . . like Doctor Fiendish."

*Doctor Fiendish?* Don't ask where that one came from. It's just scary that something so weird could have left my mouth.

He thankfully ignored it. "We ought to back up some," he said. "I used to be surprised by what supposedly normal folks are capable of doing to other folks. Sad fact is, though, I've been at my job long enough so nothing gets ruled out." He paused, shifted gears on me. "There anybody on your staff who might've had dealings with Buster?"

"Well, it seems like *everyone* around town bought cars and trucks from him . . ."

"I meant dealings of a personal nature."

McClintock's faint smile made me want to go squirming under my chair. I was an endless reservoir of perceptivity, wasn't I?

"I don't know," I said. "If somebody did, I figure he or she would've mentioned it when we booked his party. He was such a huge VIP—"

"Nashville isn't New York. It's a different world here. People have ties going back a long way. Grudges too sometimes. And they don't always talk about them."

I looked at him. "You'd know best about that sort of thing," I said. "But if one of my employees had a problem with Buster Sergeant, it's breaking news to me."

McClintock grunted, rapped out another series of beats on the desk. Then he hitched his chair forward a little, leaning closer.

"I'll need to speak with everyone at your restaurant," he said. "As I mentioned over the phone, I wanted to give you notice before I start my interviews. And before the press gets wind of this being a criminal investigation. A medical examiner's autopsy report is public record in Tennessee. We've got ways to stall its release a while with a murder case, but there are going to be leaks. Sure as we're sitting in this room, word'll get out that Buster was murdered at your delicatessen."

My eyes bulged between schmeers of lifter cream and super-concealer. I was back to imagining lurid tabloid headlines. Plural. A whole montage of them swirled around my brain like in some old Orson Welles movie.

"This is going to kill my busin—"

I cut myself off. A man was dead. How cruddy would it sound if I whined about the news stories pushing my business, my already on-life-support finances, and worst of all, Uncle Murray's dream, into the grave with Buster?

Assuming he wasn't cremated so his ashes could be scattered across one of his car lots, of course.

My head ached. I don't know how long I sat there goggling at McClintock. Maybe it was only a minute, but it felt like ten. Meanwhile, a very basic question was nagging at me. And had been since he'd phoned the restaurant.

I took a deep breath to pull myself together. It worked to a negligible extent.

"How come you told me about the report . . . and your investigation?" I asked. See? Basic.

McClintock was still leaning slightly forward, his gray eyes studying me, his fingers tapping again.

"Your uncle had a reputation for helping lots of folks in this town," he said. "I wanted to repay his generosity."

I looked at him across the desk, sensing he wasn't being altogether frank. "Maybe I'm wrong," I said, "but after speaking to my manager last night, I got the impression you knew Murray."

"Your manager."

"Yes. Thomasina Jackson. It was obvious you and *she* know each other."

McClintock met that with silence—and all the expressiveness of a bare plasterboard wall. His hands on the desk, he pushed to his feet and motioned toward his door without acknowledging my question.

"I'll be in touch soon, Gwen," he said, going over to open the door for me. "I should walk you out to the elevator."

"I can find it," I said. "Thanks, anyway, Detective Mc—"

"Beau," he said. "Please. Let's both keep it on a first name basis."

*Sure, why not?* Though I'd have appreciated it if my question hadn't seemingly bounced off deaf ears.

I nodded, turned, and stepped into the hall. In the elevator, I glanced at my watch and realized it was almost eleven o'clock. Good. Thom would be at the restaurant by now and I wanted a few words with her. My hunch was she'd try to steamroll me once I got started . . . but that would be fine.

I was just pissed enough not to care.

# Chapter Six

On my way back to the restaurant, I smoked half a Pall Mall and then detoured into a relatively new place on Fourth Avenue called Happy's Sweet Shop for emotional reinforcements—in other words, a high-voltage chocoholic charge of Three Musketeers, Butterfinger, and Baby Ruth bars. Plus a bag of Hershey's Miniatures. Oh, and a six-pack of Nestlé Crunches *naturalmente*.

"That'll be twenty-four dollars and eighty cents," said the tubby storekeeper. "Y'need a bag?"

"Yes, thanks," I said, and paid him. And then waited as he looked over my purchases.

"Don't know if I can fit all these in a single bag," he said.

"Well, how about using two bags?"

He pulled a face, nodded toward a sign on his register. Covered with transparent tape, it read: *We have reduced the number of plastic bags leaving our store to help protect the environment.*

"I try'n conserve," he told me. "Resources, y'know."

I looked at Happy, assuming he *was* Happy and not just someone who happened to work for him. While I considered myself as ecologically conscious as the next person, the load of chocolates I'd emptied from my shopping basket was roughly as high as Kilimanjaro. And anyone with a functional pair of eyes would've realized that the mini-slouch hanging from my shoulder could barely hold my cell phone, wallet, and take-along makeup kit without bulging apart at the seams.

I considered asking if I was supposed to balance everything on my head—but decided against it. This was the South. It was inhabited by polite, gracious Southerners, never mind that the man provisionally known as Happy seemed to possess none of those qualities. I would either learn to fit in or remain a displaced East Coast gefilte fish.

"Actually," I said. "I'd be very obliged if I could have those bags."

*Obliged,* I thought. *O-blee-iged. A nice, tactful Southern-sounding word.*

Happy frowned, reached under his counter, and produced a fabric sack with the name of his shop printed on it. "We sell this here tote for five dollars," he said. "It's reusable."

And free advertising. Maybe a week or two back, a salesman from a custom-tote maker had come into the deli and offered me a hundred complimentary samples, offering to put our logo on at no cost. I'd passed, figuring they didn't suit our needs.

"No, thanks," I said with a smile—and an obliging one at that. "Plastic bags are fine."

Undaunted, Happy wagged the sack in my face.

"Give you a dollar off 'cause you made a large purchase," he said. "I read somewhere how a plastic bag can blow from a picnic table, wind up in a storm drain, then wash into a river. Next thing you know, it's smotherin' an innocent seal pup in the middle a the Atlantic ocean."

I willed my smile to stay put. It wasn't easy. There was being green, and there was using it as an excuse for being cheap. "I'll stick with plastic, if you don't mind," I said.

Happy gave me a crooked look that I guessed was supposed to fill my moral cup with shame. Things were getting weird. Happy's Sweet Shop was an implicitly stress-relieving, dare I say, *happy*-sounding name for a store. Since I'd been stressing out in a major way, this had seemed like the perfect occasion to pay it a first visit. But Happy had quickly soured me on the place.

He was getting my change out of his cash drawer when I noticed the large paper shopping bags on a wall hook behind him.

"How about giving me one of those?" I said, pointing. "I'm sure that'd be enough for my candy."

He glanced over his shoulder. "They only come with our twenty-five-dollar gift boxes."

"But I just spent twenty-four eighty."

"Which is short'a twenty-five," he said. "Besides. . . ."

"You can keep the change. That'll bring me up to twenty-five even."

He shook his head. "As I was startin' to explain, ma'am, policy's policy," he said. "You didn't purchase a gift box."

That did it. Bye-bye tact. He could shove his store policy.

"Look, I want to get going," I said. "You can either put my chocolates in a couple of plastic bags or one big paper shopping bag. But you're putting them in *something* I can carry out of here without me paying an extra cent. Unless you want the whole neighborhood to know you're a squeaker."

"A what?"

"S-q-u-e-a-k-er," I said, spelling it out to him. "Not to mention a stingy, miserly jerk who's made me a very *un*happy customer."

Happy backed away, staring. I figured my angry words had surprised him. Unless maybe my eye makeup needed freshening. But it was guaranteed to last twelve hours and hadn't failed me yet.

A moment passed. Happy's face went from wearing an expression of shock and awe to . . . I couldn't tell. It definitely softened, though. "Hang on," he said. "You own that deli around the block, right?"

I nodded.

"That explains it," Happy said, sounding downright sad all of a sudden. As I tried to figure out what to make of it, he silently packed my chocolates into the plastic bags and put *both* into a shopping bag. Then he took the fabric tote he'd tried pawning off on me, carefully folded it in half, and added it to the shopping bag's contents for good measure. "Here you go, on the house." He pushed the bag into my arms. "I'm sorry."

"What's that supposed to mean?"

"Just that I'm sorry," he said, shaking his head without explanation.

I left Happy's Sweet Shop in a funk, which was *not* what I'd counted on. It was as good a reason as any for me to stop midway up the street, tear open the pack of Hershey's Miniatures, and bolt down a Crunch bar before heading back to the deli.

The front door was locked when I reached it, as it should have been with an hour to go till lunch. I didn't feel like fumbling for my keys while in schlep mode with the shopping bag, and instead walked up the alley to the side entrance. It was always open for deliveries that time of day.

The kitchen itself was empty, and I could hear my lunch crew eating out in the dining room. Anyone who's worked at a restaurant knows it's SOP to grab some chow before the place opens, and Newt's special Friday cholent had drawn everybody into the action. I had three waiters on shift—Raylene Sue Chappell, Medina Ramirez, and our headwaiter, Vernon Reeves, who boasted of having been my uncle's first hire and was ancient enough to have served Abraham and his flock their daily matzos . . . or had it been it manna?

Anyway, I went through the kitchen and pushed through the double doors, figuring I'd say hello to everyone before heading upstairs.

Normally it would've been quite the merry jamboree out there. Luke had stuck around while I was gone, and A.J., Newt and Jimmy were also at the table. But they were all kind of drooped over their bowls, and I can't say it surprised me. None of them was under the illusion that this was anything close to an ordinary day . . . except, it seemed, for Thomasina, who was making her usual deliberate inspection of the booths and tables, slowly working her way between them like a warship on patrol.

I swept past the crew with a wave, pretending not to notice Luke's concerned expression. I hadn't told him why I'd rushed off a little while ago, but he wasn't dumb, and would know it hadn't been to go on a chocolate spree—my sweet shop bounty notwithstanding.

Her back to me as I approached, Thom didn't bother to look up from a bus cart full of pickle and sauerkraut bowls that had come under her critical scrutiny.

"We need to talk," I said, halting behind her.

"Where you been?" She kept her disapproving eyes on the cart. "It's late."

"Call me unreliable," I said. And shrugged. "Go on and throw in undependable too."

Thom ignored that and nodded down at the top shelf. "What's wrong with this picture?" she grumbled.

I immediately identified the problem. You might've heard about the pickle principle that's invoked with every corporate pep talk nowadays . . . the customer wants a little something extra, you gladly provide it and win them over. Well, surprise, surprise, it's an idea that originated at Jewish delis. If you wanted satisfied diners, you doled out all the pickles they could eat and *then* some at no extra charge. At Murray's, our policy was to overwhelm people with generous servings of kosher dills—adding a spear or two to every main course that left the kitchen, filling every pickle bowl on the tables with at least a dozen whole sours and half sours in brine.

The confounding thing now was that there were only three or four pickles in each bowl.

"Where're all the dills?" I asked.

"There you have it," Thom said, still without looking in my direction. She raised her voice so it would carry to where the gang was eating lunch. "Appears somebody here skimped on 'em this morning."

Newt glanced at her over a spoonful of cholent. "Sure hope you don't mean me."

"You hear someone mention your name?"

"I'm only sayin' not to fling around accusations." He slowly ate his food. "Wouldn't want you makin' a fool of yourself, bless your heart."

She finally turned her attention from the cart, scowling at him across the room. Her snug pullover blouse had a bagel print at the breast line above the words BAGEL LOVIN' MAMA—which I noted even while refusing to consider any psychosexual inferences.

"You're nobody to toss around blessings, Newt. Or talk about anyone else's foolishness," she said. "I'll worry about who's to blame later. All I care to know now is why there ain't enough pickles in these bowls."

He grunted, plunged his spoon into his stew. "We can't put out what we don't have."

It was my turn to look at him. "Are you kidding? I ordered twenty gallons the other day."

"Right," Newt said. "And the shipment came this

ay-em. A whole skid load 'a frozen, battered pick-les." He paused, chewing again. "Pickle spears, to be perfectly accurate."

I blinked in surprise. He might as well have said we'd gotten strawberries in ketchup. Or bat-wing jelly.

"*Battered* pickle spears?"

"For deep fryin'." Newt pulled the spoon from his mouth and twirled its handle between his fingertips, staring at it contemplatively. "The supplier you called was Billy's Dillies on Sixteenth Avenue, right? Down there past the roundabout?"

I nodded. It had been another instance of my choosing a name at random out of the local business-to-business phonebook, just like when I'd ordered the pastrami that turned out to be a pig. And I'd done it for the same reason—namely that I couldn't find Murray's distributor list.

"I ordered sours and half sours," I said. "How could anybody get confused?"

"Wasn't no confusion," Newt said. "Accordin' to his truck driver, Billy was all outta stock. So he went 'n sent us the battered pickles at half price to make up for it." He shrugged. "Nothing wrong with 'em if you want a down-home treat."

"Newt," I said. "Tell me something, okay? Has a Jewish deli ever, ever, ever in a million years been considered *down home*?"

"Nope," he said. "That's why we went light with the kosher pickles we got left."

I expelled a sigh of frustration that went down to my ankles. *Batter-fried pickles.* What an incredible screwup. My mind hadn't stopped recoiling from the concept.

"I need to straighten this out," I said.

"I'd say so," Thomasina said.

"But first *we* need to talk," I said, shooting her a look.

She pursed her lips tightly. "I'm listenin'."

"No," I said. "Not here."

"Then where?"

Good question, I thought. My office was a cluttered, nerve-wracking sty. That made avoiding it imperative when I confronted her—the idea of which was sufficiently nerve-wracking in itself.

I scanned the room until my eyes settled on the kitchen doors. Feeling a burst of inspiration, I took hold of Thom's sleeve and hauled her toward them, dragging her through onto the staircase's lower landing before she could overcome her shock and wrestle free.

"Cranky, ain't you?" She frowned as the doors swung shut behind us. "You plan on hangin' onto my arm till I lose circulation?"

I let go, and she stood there rubbing it.

"Tell me what you know about an attorney named Cyrus Liarson," I said.

She abruptly stopped rubbing and fell into blockish silence, staring straight over my head.

"And while you're at it, give me the skinny on his boss Royce Ramsey," I went on.

I could have taken my time counting to ten before Thom deigned to lower her eyes to mine.

"They're the ones got you so upset?" she asked finally.

I shook my head. "No, Thom. Real-estate sharks, I can handle. What upsets me is finding out that you've spoken to Liarson. More than once. And you never bothered saying a word to me—a *single* word—about your conversations with him. Or giving me his messages."

Thomasina shrugged her shoulders.

"Guess I must've just forgot," she said. "I do apologize. Now can I get back to work?"

"Forgot?" I said with open disbelief. "Look, tell me the truth. How come you didn't want me to know about those phone calls?"

She clammed up again. I wasn't sure what to make of it . . . although I'd been harboring an ugly suspicion.

"Thom," I said, "were you trying to cut some kind of separate deal with those two predators?"

"What's that supposed to mean?"

"I repeat, you tell me," I said. "Because if you think anything will convince me to sell this restaurant . . ."

She snorted. "You got some kinda nerve makin' that vile suggestion."

"*I* do? Who's the one with the secrets here?"

Thom put her hands on her hips and thrust out her chin. "You're just loaded with questions, aren't you?"

"No. I only asked a few. And I still haven't gotten a single answer."

She held her rigid pose, but I was in no mood for her offended-diva shtick, and just stood there regarding her stonily. If Thom intended to be the immovable object, I'd be the irresistible force.

At last, she made a clucking sound with her tongue and shook her head. "I talked to Liarson, okay?" she said. "But not before talkin' to Royce Ramsey."

"Ramsey? He called you too?"

"No," she said. "He came here himself."

"Came to the *restaurant*?"

"Walked right through the front door like the devil in the flesh."

My eyes had widened. "When was this?"

"Must've been end of January, beginnin' of February."

"That's *months* ago," I said. "Around when Uncle Murray died."

"Maybe two, three days after the funeral," Thom said with a nod. "You'd come and gone back north in a blink. Right then, nobody knew he'd left you the deli or had the least notion what would happen to it. Wasn't till weeks later that we even heard he'd prepared a will."

I nodded. That whole awful period wasn't something I could've forgotten if I'd tried. The news of my uncle's fatal heart attack had struck me like lightning, coming when I was tied up with two different legal proceedings—one a final settlement hearing with my soon-to-be-ex Phil, another involving what turned out to be my final assignment with Thacker Consulting, an audit that required my appearance as a professional witness in a complicated bank fraud prosecution.

Knowing Murray would be buried within two days of his death in observance of Jewish tradition, I'd rushed to take care of my pressing affairs in

New York before I left for the funeral—huddling with federal attorneys for a long, overnight trial rehearsal in the fraud case, getting a postponement of my divorce court appearance, and booking last-minute airline reservations amidst it all. I'd flown down to Nashville in a stunned, exhausted daze, staggered through the memorial service, and cabbed directly back to the airport from the cemetery so I could be back in New York in enough time to give my expert testimony. My only conscious goal during the flight home had been to keep from sinking into an inescapable depression . . . and even now, when I could *almost* believe I'd recovered from simultaneously saying good-bye to my uncle and my marriage, my memories of the trip inevitably came in dreary shades of gray.

"I don't get it," I said. "How could Ramsey meet you at the restaurant? It closed down when Murray passed away. The very same day, in fact. And didn't reopen till after I moved down from New York last spring."

Thom frowned. "It wasn't like your uncle *warned* us he was goin' anywhere," she said. "Far as we knew, the deli was at the end of the line without him. We had reservations to cancel. And there was a kitchen full of food nobody was ever gonna eat. We had to clean the floors an' tables, empty pantries, do all manner of other jobs. Everyone who worked for Murray came and did their share . . . and I might add that not a single member of the crew expected a minute's pay."

"Is that when Ramsey showed up?" I looked

at her. "When you were here taking care of loose ends?"

"Bright an' early one morning, before the rest arrived," Thom said with a nod. "He puts his face to the door, sees me, and raps on the glass. The man struts around like a kingfish, gussied in a white suit and fancy straw hat with a feather in the band. I got no idea who he is or what he wants. But I reckon he could be one of those Music Row executive types Murray chummed around with . . . that maybe he hasn't heard Murray's passed on and wants to say hello. Or make a lunch booking, who knows?"

"So you let him in," I said.

"I did. Figured I'd give him the bad news."

"And then . . . ?"

"I find out he knows all about what happened. Calls me by name like we're old friends and expresses his condolences. Got this big, wide smile on his face, never mind anyone with two eyes in his head can see I'm torn to shreds inside."

I was silent for a moment. Thom and Uncle Murray's on-again, off-again romance may have been the worst-kept secret in Nashville since Clay Aiken's gayness—and I had a hunch someone like Ramsey would've done his due diligence. I also had a feeling I knew the reason for his visit.

"Everybody knew you were the deli's manager," I said. "He thought Murray left it to you . . . asked if you wanted to sell. Is that it?"

Thom's jaw tightened. "Far as he was concerned, it was a sure thing. 'Hear you might be looking to ease yourself of this property,' he says. Then dishes some hokum about how he'd take care of me and the staff, give us new jobs."

"And you blew him off."

"Like the crumb he is," Thom said. "It was easy, since I couldn't have sold what wasn't mine in the first place. Not that I'd have done it even if I *had* inherited the restaurant. Show me a man that smiles when he's giving his sympathies, I'll show you a honey-tongued serpent in a fruit tree."

Which mirrored my impression of his sidekick Liarson, though I might have expressed the feeling a bit differently. And which led me right back around to my original question to Thom.

I thought in silence again. Outside the kitchen doors, I could hear the rattle of silverware, bus carts rolling, chairs being pushed into place . . . the sounds of my crew preparing to open for lunch after finishing their meal together. I needed to wrap things up.

"I still don't understand why you didn't mention Ramsey's offer before. Or Liarson's follow-up calls."

She shrugged, her chin angling back upward with indignation. "I ain't the only one," she said. "Might as well ask how come nobody *else* did either."

Something inside me dropped with a hard crash. It was very possibly my heart.

"What do you mean nobody else?" I asked.

"Far as I'm aware, Liarson's talked to Newt, Vernon, and maybe Jimmy," Thom said. "He contacted them *after* you got here. Made sure they know there would be jobs for them if you decide to sell out."

I looked at her, speechless. At last I understood. And I was almost wishing I'd been able to keep my stubborn curiosity in check.

"You don't trust me," I said. "None of you."

Thom's forehead creased in another frown as she fixed her green eyes on mine. "Missy," she said. "I hope you won't take offense . . . but the honest truth is we hardly *know* you."

With that, she stepped down off the landing and pushed through the kitchen doors into the dining room. I'd meant to ask her a second set of questions about something completely unrelated to Dracula and Renfield . . . err, Ramsey and Liarson . . . but was too dejected to say another word, let alone try and stop her. Instead, I stood there alone at the bottom of the stairs, staring at the doors for a long while after they had swung shut on me.

At last, I listlessly turned and climbed the stairs to my office, put the shopping bag I'd cadged from Happy down atop a pile of cartons, and flopped into the chair behind my desk. I didn't have the gumption to unpack the bag. And as trounced as I felt, it was doubtful even chocolate comforts could cheer me up. Besides, my appetite was nonexistent.

I sighed heavily. The night before I'd been incapable of giving Goo Goo bars a fair shake. Now I was shunning my dietary staples altogether, proof positive things had gone from bad to worse.

Bummer.

Scary, scary bummer.

# Chapter Seven

Fifteen minutes later, I decided I'd maxed out on slouching around in a state of woeful depression. Sitting up reasonably straight behind the desk, I fished my cell phone from my purse and called Artemis Duff. I had asked him to update and computerize Uncle Murray's bookkeeping records—such as they were—and decided I'd might as well see how he was coming along with that almost impossible task.

"Gwennie!" he said. "I was just thinking about you."

I suddenly felt my mood lift. *Gwennie.* It was no fluke that the only other Nashvillian who'd called me that was my uncle. Murray had introduced me to him back in New York a long, long time ago.

"Must be our telepathic link," I said. "How're things? I haven't seen you at the deli in a while."

"I've been in and out. Took some books from Murray's office—sorry, *your* office. You mean Newt and Thom didn't mention it? I must've passed them four, five times the other day."

"I haven't heard a peep about an Artie sighting from them," I said. "But I did notice that some of the ledgers were moved around and figured we must have missed each other. That's why I decided to give you a ring."

"Oh." He sounded a little surprised. "I thought it was because of my e-mail. I fired one off to you this morning."

"Haven't checked my messages, to be honest. I assume you know what's been going on around here."

"It's impossible not to know."

I smiled grimly. "Guess you'd have to be somewhere out of touch with civilization, huh?"

"Way out, I'm afraid," he said. "That's why I decided to send the e-mail rather than call . . . I figured you didn't need me adding to your immediate problems."

I crinkled my forehead. "What's the matter, Art?"

He hesitated. "This is rotten timing. . . I should have waited."

My crinkles crinkled. I was certain the bags under my eyes had finally cracked my super-duper-concealing cream. It would have taken a massive Botox transfusion to do anything for them.

"Come on, Artie," I said. "Let's have it."

He paused again. "We should meet. I can be at your office in half an hour. If that works for you."

Now I was officially nervous.

"It's fine," I said. "We probably ought to talk down in the restaurant, though. Or go out somewhere for coffee. I don't have to tell you the office is a shambles right now—"

"Let's use it anyway," Artie said. "Thanks to

Murray, when I think about that office, I *think* shambles. I can pile a few cartons on top of each other and plunk down on them. It'll be like old times."

I chuckled. Artie and Murray went way back. Though Artie had been born in Tennessee, his dad had been a U.S. Army officer who moved the Duffs to Fort Dix, New Jersey when Artie was a young boy. Then around 1980 or so, he'd answered Murray's classified ad for musicians in the *Village Voice* and the pair became the Lennon-McCartney of the local country music scene. Or *could* have if there'd been a local country music scene. Which there admittedly wasn't within at least a hundred miles of the city . . . but why be nitpicky?

"See you in a little," I said, and hit the disconnect button.

Artie arrived ten minutes early with a knock on my door, not having bothered to ask anyone on my crew to show him upstairs. I let him in, and he put down his briefcase so we could exchange warm hugs. Then he went about hauling boxes over to my desk for his makeshift chair.

Concerned as I'd been that he was bringing me more bad news, Artie's presence was still welcome . . . maybe because my first memories of him were so deeply bound to my uncle. When we met I'd been in my early teens, and Artie, who was probably fifteen years older, had been playing with the band. I remembered him as a lean, bookish guy with short, dark brown hair and wire-rimmed glasses who always wore a blazer, slacks, and loafers—not your typical image of a drummer, but *exactly* what you'd expect from an accountant.

Nowadays Artie's hair was a salt-and-peppery gray, his face was a little plumper, and his waistline had broadened with middle age. But he still wore his customary laid-back outfit and, all things considered, didn't really look that different.

It would've been very easy—and wrong—to think his conservative appearance meant he'd been less of a talented and dedicated musician than Murray. But I did feel it hinted at his far greater pragmatism . . . a very important attribute as it turned out, since it was fair to say my uncle would eventually owe a club-sandwich-sized portion of his success to him.

The truth was that Murray didn't have it within him to consider what he would do if his musical career fizzled. He'd have pursued his dream at a full gallop even if it meant hurtling straight over a cliff into the abyss . . . and never, *ever* in a million years had gotten the idea to buy the property that Royce Ramsey was so eager to get his big, fat, groping entrepreneurial mitts on. It was Artie who'd kept suggesting he open a restaurant as a fallback, Artie who kept his eyes and ears open for the right location, Artie who'd helped my uncle secure the venture capital for getting the deli off the ground . . .

And Artie, I thought, who'd always kept track of his financial affairs.

"Well," I said, sitting at my desk. "Here we are."

"Yep, Gwennie," he said, clearing his throat. "We definitely are here."

We looked at each other. He'd picked his briefcase up off the floor, set it on his lap, and started fiddling with its handle.

"Artie," I said, "it's good to see you. I mean it. But you are making me uptight."

"I am?"

"Extremely," I said.

He stared at his hands as they played with the briefcase handle. They suddenly froze as if having been caught in an act of insubordination. "Sorry," he said. "I get fidgety."

So I'd noticed. "Artie?"

"Yes?"

"I asked what was wrong over the phone."

"Right."

"And you answered that you wanted to discuss it in person."

"Yes . . ."

"Which is why you came," I said. "Isn't that so?"

Artie looked at me. "Definitely, definitely—"

"Well, then, let's discuss."

His eyes were on mine. He opened his mouth, closed it, opened and closed it again, swallowed. All without a peep.

"Artie . . ."

"Murray was having money problems," he said, finally getting out the words. "His personal spending was well in excess of the income he drew from the restaurant . . . and it had put him in a spot."

"A spot."

"Right," Artie said. "A tight one."

"Tight meaning . . ."

"His mortgage, credit cards, taxes . . . he was

behind in all his payments. Months and months behind."

I considered that a second. It wasn't breaking news to me that Uncle Murray lived larger than he could afford. When I was a kid, my dad was always on his back about it—and about his fondness for betting on sports. "Artie, I understand about the spending," I said. "But as far as the restaurant . . . I thought that was where you came in. That you kept a lookout over its finances."

"I did," he said. "To the extent that I could manage."

I tried to digest that. "What are you saying? When Murray would call me in New York—I'd hear from him like clockwork every year on my birthday—he always seemed proud of how well this place was doing. I only ever heard him gripe when he talked about catered events."

"That old bugaboo," Artie said. "So he'd give you earaches about them too, huh?"

"It wasn't like he'd bring it up all the time. But, yeah, he'd complain sometimes."

"To you and me both." He gave out with a wistful chuckle. "Kosher Karaoke night was a pet peeve."

"Did he ever explain why?"

"His grumbling wasn't always logical from my perspective. As best I could follow, it had something to do with the discount rates and the type of food and drinks he'd have to provide." Artie spread his hands. "Engagements, wedding receptions, showers, anniversaries . . . and then your corporate parties, of course . . . Murray tolerated them because they'd bring in potential new customers. But he felt special events in general were loss leaders."

"Would the earnings versus expense lines reflect that?"

"I never knew for sure. The online payment system didn't help. Not with the way Murray kept his records. In fact, I'm missing a bunch of those catering files . . . which is to say I never got hold of them. My guess is they're buried somewhere in here."

I shook my head. "This is so confusing," I said. "His estate lawyers led me to believe the deli was turning a solid profit."

"And it should have been." He made a kind of broad, inclusive gesture at the office around us. "This place is so far beyond a shambles I don't have words to describe it. Accounts payable, accounts receivable . . . do you really think your uncle, God rest his soul, was capable of staying organized?"

"Not as most members of the human race know and understand the word," I said. "It's the reason I figured you'd done it for him. That you wrote stuff down in nice, ruled columns for pedestrian types like us who actually *need* to see it on paper."

"I did." Artie sighed. "Getting him to follow my procedures was another story, though. I just couldn't convince him. He had no clue who he owed money. By the same token, he had customers running up house tabs that were years past due. Running a successful business isn't just about what you take in. It's about cash flow. And he was totally neglectful."

He paused. "You know about the shoebox under the counter, right?"

I shook my head no.

"Murray was the softest touch, Gwennie. Especially when it came to struggling performers. Maybe because of his own past experiences, he couldn't resist anybody trying to make it outside the nine-to-five world. Musicians, artists, athletes . . . you'd never hear him say no when they came to him for help, or even insist on being repaid within a reasonable period."

"And where does the shoebox come in?"

"There'd be at least five hundred dollars in it on any given night, and I can tell you that's an absolute minimum," Artie said. "Murray kept it on the shelf below the cash register, and if a musician he knew said he needed a hand—whether because he couldn't afford to string his guitar or pay his rent and utilities—you can bet your uncle would reach into the box. Add all that generosity to his operating expenses and his debts became unsustainable."

Artie fell silent and went back to fooling around with his briefcase handle. It occurred to me that his expression was now out-glumming mine by a wide margin.

"How'd he manage to stay afloat for so long?" I asked. "It beats me that he could've done it without paying attention to what was coming in or going out."

Artie shrugged his shoulders. "I guess you could say he had a knack," he said. "You're probably too young to appreciate the comparison, but he reminded me of the plate spinners I used to watch on the Ed Sullivan Show. One guy, an Italian circus performer, I remember he'd have a high, narrow pole balanced on his forehead, another two on his shoulders, a bunch more on the floor. There'd be plates whirling on top of them, and when one started to wobble, he'd give it a fresh spin, then move to the next one, and the next, and the next after that . . . and somehow, don't ask me his secret, he'd manage to keep them from crashing down around him and breaking into smithereens."

I sat there shaking my head. The picture Artie was drawing was worse than I'd expected. "Do you have a financial workup I can see?" I said.

He nodded and started to open his briefcase. "I figured you'd want one. I'm told you're no slouch in the accounting department."

"You mean it?"

Artie paused with his hands on the latches. He seemed confused. "Sure . . . why do you ask?"

"I've gotten the feeling that people around here don't know or care anything about my background. Thomasina seems to think I was shipped straight from the pampered princess factory."

"Don't let her fool you." He flapped a dismissive hand. "Murray would always brag about your Wall Street consulting work. To hear it from him, you should've been put in charge of the national treasury. And if I heard it, she did too. Probably more because they spent so much time together."

A smile touched my lips. "I suppose," I said, and stuck my chin out at his briefcase. "What is it you were just getting from in there?"

He looked back down at it as if suddenly reminded, snapped open the lid, and removed a large brown padded envelope. "I copied my charts," he said, holding it out. "I have paper printouts, a CD, whatever you prefer."

I took the envelope from his hand. "Thanks, Artie. I'll give them a look."

"The account listings are grouped by assets and liabilities," he said. "It's pretty basic stuff compared to what you were used to evaluating in New York."

I set the envelope down on the desk between us and sat there in silence awhile. Then I noticed him shifting around on his ad hoc stool. "That pile of boxes looks really uncomfortable," I said, glancing at my watch to discover it was already lunchtime. "You sure you don't want to join me for coffee downstairs? Or maybe a bite to eat? It's fresh cholent day in case you forgot."

"How could I? My back's achy but my nose is working fine," Artie said with a grin. "Much as you've tempted me, I have a full plate of things to do this weekend . . . you'll forgive the expression." He stretched a little, massaging the base of his spine. "Guess all those years I'd sit hunched over a drum kit took its toll."

Smiling faintly again, I got up, walked Artie through the obstacle course of cardboard boxes between us and the door, then accompanied him into the short hall off the second-story landing.

He was sharing some parting thoughts when I found myself momentarily distracted by something on the floor below. Or rather by its absence.

"Gwennie, you okay?" he asked.

I snapped, my attention drifting back to him, embarrassed. "Sorry, I've been a total scatterbrain since last night."

Artie made a sympathetic face. "Don't apologize. I realize I've dumped a lot on your shoulders, and that you had enough of a load beforehand," he said. "I have to ask, though . . . have you considered what you're going to do next?"

I shrugged. "Dunno, Artie. Buy a dozen lottery tickets maybe?"

It was a joke, people. I repeat, a joke. Not that hitting the million-dollar jackpot wouldn't have solved a great many of my problems.

Artie smiled, and I smiled back, neither of us looking too amused as we turned to go our separate ways.

# Chapter Eight

Artie had no sooner turned into the kitchen than I decided I'd head down to the restaurant too . . . though I guess he must have left through the side door, because he was gone before I reached the bottom of the stairs.

I'd lied moments earlier when giving him the reason for my divided attention. It had nothing to do with being scattered noggin-wise, and everything to do with the silence below us. Thanks to Murray's cholent, Saturday always had been the busiest lunch day of the week, filling the place to capacity. That typically meant waves of noise from rattling dishes, clinking glasses and silverware, and most of all customers enjoying themselves.

Silence never boded well in an eatery. And it seemed an even more ominous sign in view of the morning headlines about Buster Sergeant.

Taking a deep breath, I pushed through the kitchen doors and stood looking out over the empty dining floor.

Empty, that is, aside from a very disconsolate

staff headed by Thomasina Jackson. Frowns on their faces, they were all staring at the deli's entrance like wax figures in some mournful abandoned gallery. Old Vernon, the waiter, was the only one who was remotely animated, if you could use that word to describe his rubbing a rag over an already spotless tabletop.

"Lucky thing this bunch here can eat bigger than horses at hay time . . . me excluded," Thom said, turning to face me from where she stood near the door. "Would've been a shame if Newt's cookin' went to waste 'cause nobody else in town has any kind of appetite."

"For *our* food anyway," Vern said without raising his head. "Unless, I suppose, all Nashville's gone on a strict calorie count today."

"Yeah," Thom said. "How about we call it Buster Sergeant's Drop Dead Diet?"

I frowned. "That isn't funny," I said.

"Who's jokin'?" Thom said. She gestured toward the front door. "What do you see when you look outside, Nash?"

Regardless of whether she'd meant it to be rhetorical, the question needed no answer. The bright, beautiful early summer morning had turned into an equally perfect day, and Broadway was hopping with foot traffic.

"Maybe we ought to get the exhaust fan blowing out of the kitchen so people can smell the food," Luke said. "I hear that's a good way to bring them in off the street."

Thom scowled. "Well, Luke, aren't you a genius? I'm thrilled you finally got that trick figured out. I mean, now that we been doin' it ever since you was wigglin' around your nursery room in skintight diapers—"

"Okay, enough, give it a rest." I chopped my right hand against my left palm. "This bickering won't help if there's a problem."

"If?" Vern had finally raised his eyes from the tabletop, a hangdog look on his face. "We gotta face facts, Nash. The restaurant is doomed."

I turned to him, my mouth gaping open. "*Doomed?* How can you say that? Just because one man passed away here last night . . ."

"A famous man everybody round this way knows, loves, and respects."

"Okay, granted," I said. "To qualify, just because a man I will freely concede everybody in Nashville is crazy about happened to die here . . ."

"Under suspicious circumstances," Vern interrupted again. "Which, I heard on my car radio, might have to do with our meat bein' spoiled."

I looked at him. Spoiled, no way. Injected with outlawed coyote poison? Eh, maybe. But if the police were right about that, and Buster Sergeant had been specifically targeted for murder, it only went to confirm there was nothing wrong with our quality control. And that anybody whose name *wasn't* Buster was probably good to go for lunch. "Vern . . . do you actually believe it could happen a second time?"

"What he thinks don't count," Thom said. "Neither does what you, I, or anyone else in this place thinks." She jabbed her chin in the direction of the busy sidewalk. "It's whatever they think out there that counts enough for all of us put together. And I can hardly blame them for stayin' away. Folks hereabouts have managed to get over your uncle bein' gone. But when worse news piles on top of bad news, and every bit's associated with Murray's deli, it's natural for 'em to seek out another place to eat."

I was shaking my head in frustration. "This is unbelievable," I said, looking around at my staff. "My God . . . what are we, a bunch of *quitters*?"

"Quitters this, quitters that . . . and would you please stop usin' His name in vain?" Thom said. "Like Vern was tellin' you, we got to face reality. And from what I can see—"

*"Hola!"* Medina Ramirez blurted in Spanish. A short, dark-haired woman of generous proportions, she'd stood quietly near a booth, her arms folded across her middle. But now she was suddenly gesticulating past me at the door. "Is foxes!"

*Is foxes?* I had trouble deciphering Medina's broken English even when she was calm and making nominal sense. But right at that moment I had no clue what she was talking about.

I turned toward the front of the restaurant, looking straight up the center aisle . . . and all at once felt something on my face that had been missing in action since before the karaoke disaster—namely a smile. And not just any smile, but a big, unrestrained, happity-hap-happy highbeam of a smile. Foxes, of course! With everything that had been on my mind, it was no wonder I'd temporarily forgotten about them.

Still grinning from ear to ear, I hurried toward the door to welcome my diners. *Happity-hap-happy, yahoo!*

# Chapter Nine

"Why's everybody so down in the dumps?" asked Mary Ann Fox, leading her group through the door. "I didn't see a sign in the window about a wake!"

I should mention that a group of foxes is properly called a *skulk,* though I'm not sure Mary Ann would have been enthused with the term, being that she and the women who'd arrived with her definitely weren't accustomed to skulking around anywhere. On the contrary, they came, they saw, and they strutted.

Also, while I'm on a language kick, there's also no righter time to clarify that Medina had meant to use the term "*Silver* Foxes"—as opposed to just plain "foxes"—when she'd been pointing excitedly at the door a few seconds before. Besides being a brutal syntax scrambler, she was a habitual word whacker.

Mary Ann Fox, then, was the founder and leader of the Silver Foxes. A group of women rather than bushy-tailed animals of the sort Johnny Weir occasionally sported on his shoulder while skating.

I won't harp on my inability to understand half of what left Medina's mouth. Her grasp of the language was shaky at best, but as a Mexican immigrant she had a natural excuse. More so than A.J., for instance, who wasn't too understandable herself most of the time . . . and *she'd* been born and raised in the great American state of Tennessee.

Now I took a quick head count of the women behind Mary Ann and saw that over twenty had accompanied her. They included the rest of the club's core four—Somerset Vaughn, Frances DePaul, and Loretta "Lolo" Baker, all of whom had introduced themselves to me at Uncle Murray's memorial service.

*Twenty,* I thought. The size of the roster pleasantly overwhelmed me.

"Mary Ann," I said, walking up to greet her. "I had no idea your group was coming in."

"Isn't it Saturday, darling?"

"Yes . . ."

"And didn't I tell you at Murray's sendoff that we hold our weekly luncheon here *every* Saturday?"

I nodded. The funeral was largely a blur, but I did recall it. "We're really delighted to see you," I said, hoping she hadn't mistaken my surprise for something negative. "It's just that, well, we . . ."

My sentence petered out. What was I supposed to say? That a minute ago my entire staff had been wondering if anyone would ever walk through the door again, period?

Instead, I motioned her toward the dining area. "We can seat you at booths or tables . . . take your pick, there are several available," I said. As if she couldn't see for herself that the place was empty as the Bates Motel *after* the shower scene. "If you prefer, we'll push a few of the tables together—"

"TSF always takes tables. Booths ain't their style!"

*TSF?* Forget my surprise that the group rated an acronym. I owed the sudden unwanted, unnecessary, and overbearing interruption to Thom, who'd come charging up the aisle, pushed past me toward the group of women, and taken Mary Ann's hand into both of hers. "How y'all been?" she asked.

"Spectacular," Mary Ann said. "I was just explaining to Murray's lovely niece—"

"Call me Gwen, please," I said.

Mary Ann flashed me a buoyant smile. "I was about to let darling Gwen know that once the four of us—Somer, Frances, Lolo and I—heard about last night's frightfulness, we couldn't wait to lend our support to the delicatessen."

I gave her an appreciative look. "That's very kind of you, Mary Ann."

"It seemed to us people might shy away from here after reading the newspaper stories. Which plain wouldn't make sense."

"None whatsoever. But it's very considerate of you anyway . . ."

"Don't mention it." She flapped a hand. "Course, my girls do love murder mysteries. We discuss them here at every gathering of the club."

"New *books,* that is," said one of the women who'd entered behind her. Fiftyish, slim, and wearing a pink floral print dress, she nudged closer in the aisle. "I don't know if you recognize me . . . we met at your uncle's funeral service. I'm—"

"Lolo," I said, taking her hand. How could I have *forgotten* a name like that? "It's great to see you."

"And under better circumstances this time." She frowned. "Well, not entirely better, I suppose. Since yet another poor man of your acquaintance has dropped dead, and right here in the restaurant. But what I meant to say was we love reading mysteries, and sometimes even schedule mystery *writers* to appear at the library. Mary Ann's late husband, may he rest in peace, was a Rutherford County sheriff's detective. She's too modest to say it, but *I* can tell you he owed his entire career to their talking shop at the breakfast table."

"Lolo, that's way too much praise," Mary Ann said, clearly basking in its glow. "True, I might've nudged Brandon in the proper direction once or twice during an investigation. But Lolo can tell you how good she is at clues . . . she has an unusual flair for noticing things that aren't where they belong." She smiled at Lolo. "What's that expression you always use, sweetie?"

"Anything out of place is a case!" Lolo said.

Mary Ann clapped her hands and laughed. "I do *so* love it."

Cute. I felt my temples twang and wished I could stuff a cigarette in my mouth, though I'd have gladly accepted a five-mil Valium as consolation. Grateful as I was for their turnout, these women were driving me to distress. And to think I'd been happily *yahooing* about a minute ago.

"How about we get everyone seated?" I said,

motioning toward the rear. "We have all sorts of Saturday lunch specials. Uncle Murray's cholent, our Full of Bologna sandwich, Johnny Cashew pie for dessert . . ."

Those items had barely rolled off my tongue when the Silver Foxes started filing past me into the restaurant. To my immense relief, they were soon eying menus at their tables, where Vernon and Medina had doubled up to help them. I'd needed a break from discussing Buster Sergeant or anything connected to his murder.

It buoyed me when over half the ladies decided to try the Full of Bologna, a sandwich Uncle Murray must have fixed hundreds of times back home in Long Island, but for some reason never made one of the deli's offerings. As we'd prepared for our grand reopening, I was astounded to learn that not even Newt had heard of it, and will admit I'd gotten a kick out of rectifying that conspicuous omission, insisting it be included with our other lunch staples, and demonstrating its simple preparation to Newt almost exactly as Uncle Murray had shown me. . . .

*"First you sauté the onions till they're transl— uh, what's the word again Gwennie . . . ?"*

*"Translucent."*

*"That's it. You don't want them getting brown. Use a nice big frying pan or grill and just enough oil to cover the bottom so the onions and bologna won't stick. Once the onions are ready, you add the bologna slices and cook them till they pop up sorta*

*like army helmets. Then you turn them over with a
fork or tongs—be careful not to tear 'em—and do
the other side so it bulges too. Now . . . you got
some hard rolls cut for the next step?"*

*"Right here, Uncle Murray . . ."*

*"Deli mustard from the fridge, I hope."*

*"Is there any other kind for a hearty sandwich?"*

*"Atta girl! What you're gonna do after the
bologna's done frying is stack it so that . . ."*

". . . they're right in the kitchen," Lolo Baker was
saying to me.

I realized I'd slipped off into a daydream about
Murray as I went from table to table asking my
guests if they were satisfied with everything. I felt
instant embarrassment—it was unlike me to go
through the motions.

"I'm sorry, Lolo," I said from behind her. "What
was that again? I must've phased out for a second."

"Not to worry, sugar," she said, reaching out to
pat my wrist. "After what you've been through
since last night, it's a marvel you aren't in a worse
state."

"Guess I'm a little overtired," I said, hardly thinking that was an excuse. "I still appreciate you being
so understanding."

Lolo gave my wrist another pat or two. She was
a trim, patrician woman in her fifties who'd reput-
edly married well many times over, and her short
blond cut put her among the small minority of
Silver Foxes to be acquainted with hair dye, since

most had silvery coifs . . . hence the first part of the club's name, oh magnificent Carnac.

"You ought to repeat your comment about those stairs, Lolo," Somer Vaughn said. "I'm surprised none of us ever noticed it before. I reckon it's that sense you have for things being in their right places. Or wrong ones."

Lolo was shrugging. "Somer here's always playing detective. Though she's got a nose for it, I admit."

Somer shooshed her off. "Stop," she said. "There you go with your stories again."

"Is that right?" Frances laughed. "Remember way back when we heard about that Jose Menendez fella and his wife getting shot in their living room? I can picture us in front of the television like it was yesterday. They said on the news their sons called the police, and you turned to me and asked, 'Now why'd those two nice-lookin' boys do that to their mama and daddy?' And then there was the time with that football player . . ."

"That's enough from the two of you, *please,*" Somer said. "Go on, Lolo. The stairs. What was it about them you found odd?"

"It's nothing more than a minor curiosity," she told me. "I happened to see Vern turn into the kitchen, and noticed them behind the doors. First time they ever caught my eye . . . it's an unusual spot for them, isn't it?"

"Kinda," I said. "It was something they had to work around during the building's renovation. But it's convenient too."

"Oh?"

I nodded. "The steps lead up to my office. So I can take a shortcut through the alley when I'm in a hurry."

Lolo looked as if she had another question on her mind, but Mary Ann interrupted us before she could ask it.

"Excuse our annoying questions," she said. "We want to support our favorite restaurant and get to the bottom of this nasty episode with Buster Sergeant. Crime-solving's what we do—we can't help ourselves."

I blinked as her words registered. I didn't see how she could have known about the poisoning.

"Crime?" I said. "What do you mean?"

"Well, you know, it's only guesswork right now," Mary Ann said with a smile. "My forte's getting to the bottom of TV crimes . . . I guarantee you *don't* want to sit next to me when there's a police drama on, because I'm bound to spoil the end. But those stories aren't all that different from real-world incidents, and it's surely odd that the police haven't yet made a public statement about what killed poor ol' Buster."

I decided to carry on the ignorance-is-bliss routine, which meant pretending McClintock hadn't tipped me off that the police department's silence was very deliberate . . . and that the medical examiner's report was being kept under wraps.

"Maybe they just don't *know* why he died," I said. "After all, it's been less than twenty-four hours. . . ."

"Gwen, honey, listen," Mary Ann said. "In your experience, has there ever been a time when a bigshot—or even some poor average fella who winds up in the news—passes away of natural causes and the papers don't give some hint about what's happened?"

I looked at her. "I suppose I never paid attention to it before," I said more or less truthfully.

"Well, take it from us," Mary Ann said. "They might not know for sure why someone's gone to meet his Maker, but if there's nothing suspicious, you can bet you'll read words like 'suspected heart attack' or 'possible stroke' or some such . . . isn't that right, girls?"

There were nods around the table.

"When I see the expression 'undetermined cause,' I dare say the tip of my nose *does* start to twitch," Somer said. "To me, that might as well say there's been a suicide, murder, or accident involving some famous person. Like Tiger Woods smacking his car into a fire hydrant."

"Eldrick T. Woods according to the police report," Mary Ann said, swallowing a bite of her sandwich. "At least they bothered filling in his real name after he hit a tree with the car."

"And then got his rear windshield smashed to pieces," Frances said.

"And his head cracked open," Lolo said.

"And his teeth knocked loose," Somer said. "Before he wound up laying on the ground unconscious for six minutes."

"Unconscious and bleeding out of his mouth," Mary Ann said.

"Not that anyone could have hit him or his car with a golf club," Frances said.

"Oh no, no, no," Lolo said. "Not Eldrick!"

"Six minutes from undetermined causes!" Somer said.

"How dare people spread those *atrocious* rumors about Eldrick getting bashed in the head!" Mary Ann exclaimed.

I was quiet as the women broke out into trills of laughter. Besides making me wonder if being named Eldrick could lead to lifelong psychosexual issues—assuming it was an actual, honest-to-God name—the Silver Foxes' recreational sleuthing had confirmed that the warning McClintock had given me at his office was on the mark. If *they* could glean there was more to the Buster Sergeant story than the Nashville police had let on, and do it literally overnight, then I was certain the media would be savvy enough to pick up on it.

"Darling, I should mention that I *love* the salad that comes with this sandwich," Mary Ann said, her laughter subsiding now. She motioned to her plate with her fork. "It's so fresh and delectable."

Murray would've appreciated her compliment, I thought. It echoed the exact words he'd spoken when he unveiled his Full of Bologna to me. *"Don't forget, Gwennie. Always serve these babies with sliced cherry tomatoes. Sprinkle them with parsley and coarse salt and you can't go wrong. The idea is to keep things fresh and simple."*

I stood there at the core four's table another minute, then moved on to continue my rounds and welcome the rest of the group's members. Frankly, though, I was already looking past lunch to when the deli closed for a couple of hours as we prepared for the dinner crowd . . . assuming we *drew* a crowd. The break would give me a chance to spend some time upstairs in the office, where I meant to confront the daunting challenge of going through the boxes Uncle Murray had left around. There were a whole lot of unexplained questions about how Murray had apparently plummeted into financial quicksand . . . far, far too many for my liking.

McClintock and the Silver Foxes could tackle the questions hovering over Buster Sergeant's demise, and I would be nothing but appreciative. Thanks to them, I'd been inspired to do some detective work of my own—sticking to what I knew best.

It was time I started looking for answers in the numbers.

# Chapter Ten

"What in the Sam Hill is goin' *on* here?" Thomasina said from my doorway.

Crouched over an open carton on the floor, I somehow refrained from asking what the hell "what in the Sam Hill" was supposed to mean. Instead, I pulled a manila folder out of the box.

"I'm getting things organized," I said. One of those expanding-accordion types, the folder was so thick with files it was ready to burst at the seams. "Or hadn't you noticed Murray left the office just a *smidge* on the untidy side?"

Thom's lips turned down toward her chin. Well, that's not quite correct. They'd already been turned town when she asked her question. So let's say they turned further down.

"You can't resist givin' me a hard time, can you?" she said.

"Actually, it'd be my pleasure," I said. "We can even rewind about ten seconds. You step back outside and ask if I need help . . . knocking's optional incidentally. Then *I* look up, smile, and say I'd really appreciate a hand. Hard time canceled. And the next thing you know we're working together in harmony to put this mess in order."

I heard air blast from her nostrils and gathered my suggestion didn't enthuse her.

"You wanted me to add up the lunch receipts and I done it," she said, displaying the tally sheet. "Can I set this someplace to your princessly likin'?"

"Put it down anywhere in this junk heap and it's bound to go the way of the woolly mammoth."

"Huh?"

"You know . . . like in the La Brea tar pits?"

She gave me a blank look.

"Siberia ring a bell?" I said.

Blankness continued to reign on her face.

"Never mind," I said. "Look . . . why don't you just read off the totals?"

Thom shrugged. "Good enough," she said. "I wasn't sure you'd trust me after our exchange of words this morning."

Righto. As if I'd been the one to deliberately conceal the truth about having heard from Royce Ramsey. "Read away," I said. "I'm all ears."

"We took in four hundred twenty-seven dollars cash money, and another three hundred and five in charges," Thom said, glancing down at the sheet. "The grand total's seven hundred thirty-two dollars."

"And what was the average Saturday lunch take before Murray died . . . just an estimate?"

"I'd say a thousand dollars, plus or minus."

"So we're down by three hundred dollars—less

than a third the usual amount," I said. "That doesn't seem too shoddy under the circumstances."

"Exceptin' the king-sized version of the Silver Foxes probably accounted for about *five hundred* all by themselves, and most of those ladies ain't regulars," Thom said. "You look at it that way, it beats a hard kick in the pants, but doesn't make me want to call in the fiddlers for a wingding."

I mulled that a few seconds and concluded it was difficult to quarrel with her. "About the customers . . . how many of the rest were familiar faces?"

"Apart from the Foxes?"

"Right."

"Wasn't a whole lot," Thom said. "Ten or so to my eyes."

I sighed. That definitely did not give me cause for celebration. "There's no getting around the drop-off in business," I said.

"Afraid not," Thom said. She put the tally sheet on my desk. "I could've told you as much without this piece of paper. When I passed through the kitchen, I saw a whole crock full of leftover cholent . . . and that says everything you'd need to know."

I frowned. Across the room, Thom stared at me, troubled. "We're in bad shape, ain't we?" she said. "Putting aside the afternoon receipts."

I looked into her face, standing up among the jumble of cartons. I wasn't about to sugarcoat things. "Artie Duff says my uncle's finances were a worse disaster than this office. According to him, the restaurant might've been doing brisk business, but was still hemorrhaging money."

"How could that be?"

"I wish I knew," I said, and paused to think. "You wouldn't have any idea where Murray kept his online catering records, would you?"

She shook her head and made a pushing gesture. "I stayed clear a that whole computer orderin' thing," she said. "It was way too complicated for me."

"Artie felt the same . . . and he's a trained accountant."

Her face pinched. "You mean it wasn't his idea to begin with?"

"No. Well, check that. I don't know *whose* idea it was," I said. "Why do you ask?"

"No reason," she said. "I just figured Artie would've had some part in it."

"I suppose it's possible. He sure didn't seem thrilled with how the system was set up—but I know from my own accounting experience that it's easier to brainstorm a system like that than implement it," I said. "Anyway, I'd like to dig up those files. Artie thinks they might be here somewhere."

Thomasina's face had continued to tighten with concern. "Princess, with all this confusion, you tellin' me we won't make it?"

"Until we see what's in these cartons, I won't know what to tell you. And even then, it might be impossible to get everything sorted out. Maybe if I can untangle Murray's personal losses from the profits he took in here . . ."

I let the sentence trail. There'd been something else on my mind with regard to my uncle.

She looked at me. "What is it?"

I hesitated. "Thom, tell me . . . did Murray ever have trouble getting food deliveries?"

She huffed out a laugh. "Lawsy, lawsy no."

*Lawsy, lawsy?* I desperately needed a Southern slang dictionary. Although it seemed to me a good, long smoke would be a great alternative. "Then you don't remember a situation like we had last night?"

"With that hog Luke picked up at the airport?"

"Right."

Thom shook her head. "I guarantee you," she said, "if we'd of got a pig instead of a pastrami, Murray would've slaughtered it a second time before lettin' its baked butt into his kitchen."

"And how about the pickle shortage?"

"It'd be like a church hall bingo game without lonely hearts widows."

*"What?"*

"There'd be no chance."

"So these kinds of things never happened before," I said. "To the best of your knowledge."

"Mine or anyone else's."

"How about with our restaurant services? Were kitchen or dining room supplies ever late to arrive?"

"No."

"Linens?"

"Always came back from the cleaners on time," she said. And looked right into my eyes. "Okay, Princess, my turn. You prepping me for a quiz or is there some other cause for this drill?"

I realized I was on the brink of a sharing moment. Or is "moment of sharing" the phrase? The point being that I hadn't counted on having one with

Thom any more than I'd contemplated jumping in front of a speeding locomotive. But I could suddenly see its headlights bearing down on me . . . and they looked conspicuously like her unwavering blue eyes.

"I'm only trying to confirm something to myself," I said. "When Murray was trying to make it as country musician in New York, his mother— my grandmother—constantly discouraged him from sticking with it. He was almost thirty-five years old and music was all he cared about besides cooking, which he considered his hobby. He'd dropped out of college when he was eighteen, worked a zillion odd jobs so he could buy his instruments and set up his own studio. But she never let up on telling him he should've been a dentist. That he could've been driving around in a Jaguar instead of some old Ford Fairmont."

"Bet he'd get plenty upset."

I nodded. "They'd have the worst blowouts. And I'm talking at family occasions. He'd tell her he was proud of what he did for a living even if he had to struggle to make ends meet. It was, like, '*You* pick at people's rotten teeth with your fingers! I'll use mine to pick at my guitar strings!'"

Thomasina's features appeared to soften. It might've been my imagination, but I doubted it. "How 'bout the rest of the family?" she said. "You mean to say none of 'em believed in him?"

"They basically feared the wrath of Mom. Or that's how it seemed to me, though I admit I was pretty young back then. But I remember everyone running for cover when she roared."

"Includin' your dad?"

"I have to admit he was the favorite son. Went to school, got a business degree, the whole deal." I shook my head. "I guess I'm rambling, Thom. But I always felt Murray was special. That he had these *gifts.* He used to tell me he'd have been lost if he couldn't play his music and then relax by putting together a meal. . . ."

"And he was sharp as a tack when it came to such things," Thomasina said. "Murray could leave his bedroom in the morning wearin' his shirt inside out and his underpants on backwards . . . well, that is . . ."

She stopped talking, cleared her throat as if something were caught in it.

"You okay?" I asked

"Fine." She coughed into her hand. "I just didn't want to give you the notion I ever *saw* his bedroom."

"Wouldn't have occurred to me, Thom," I lied.

"Or, you know, his *drawers*."

"Of course not."

"My comment about them bein', you know . . ."

"A figure of speech."

"Right, there you have it." Thom coughed again. "What I was gettin' at is that Murray did seem scrambled sometimes. Catch him before he had his fourth cup a morning coffee, you'd have thought he was a sleepwalker. But I know he was on top a everything that went on hereabouts."

Which summed up many of the thoughts that had been circling through my head since Artie's visit. Sure, my uncle had enjoyed the high life.

Yeah, he'd had his vices. And maybe he *did* occasionally leave the house with his drawers in a twist, though I suspected Thom might have done some of the twisting herself, a mental image I preferred not to contemplate. But it seemed wrong to peg him as wasteful or oblivious to money matters just because he hadn't been good at keeping conventional records.

People had underestimated Murray pretty much his entire life. I knew he was a perfectionist about his music, and had sensed he was the same with the deli. It didn't seem likely he could've been too lax when it came to running it—not when it was obvious there was no problem paying his employees, filling his orders, and so on. In his own right-brained way, he'd seemed to have a system, or, more like it, multiple systems, of organizing his personal and professional affairs. The tricky part was that he didn't often bother sharing them with anyone.

I frowned contemplatively. It had occurred to me that if there was one thing that might have thrown those systems out of whack, it was my uncle's unlimited generosity.

"What about the cash entertainer types borrowed from Murray?" I said. "You think all those outstanding loans could've tapped him out?"

Thom screwed up an eye as if looking at me through a rifle scope. "How'd you know about them loans?"

"From Artie Duff," I said. "When he was up in my office before lunch."

"He mention the shoebox under the register?"

"Yeah," I said. "According to him, it was bottomless for musicians trying to make it in the industry."

She shook her head. "Well, he can say whatever he wants, that ain't quite the way it was."

"It isn't?"

"I just said so, didn't I?"

I waited for her to explain, and instead got about ten seconds of dead silence. "Look," I said. "Could you please help me feel less like I'm pulling teeth? For a *single* conversation?"

Thom gave a huge shrug while letting out an equally massive breath. "You'd have to know Murray like I knew him to understand," she said at last. "Just 'cause he was a kind, bighearted soul don't mean he was anybody's fool."

"So he did reach into the shoebox often enough."

"And knew darned well who'd pay him back and who wouldn't," Thom said. "Maybe he got in over his head with that computer caterin' business. But he knew people. If he didn't think someone was good for the money, he'd give what he could freely spare without figuring he'd ever see it again. For him it was the same as a charitable donation."

"What if he thought a person *would* repay him?"

"He'd dig deeper," Thom said, still beading in on me. "But he hardly ever made the wrong calls. Of all the men and women Murray helped over the years, I can't remember more'n a couple he expected to settle up that turned out to be deadbeats." She frowned. "Now it's somethin' else entirely whether he got the thanks he deserved from people . . . and by the bye, he didn't only give a leg up to musicians."

"Right," I said. "Artie mentioned something about artists. Athletes too, I guess—"

She chopped a hand through the air between us. "Let's not go there."

"Huh? I—"

"I don't want to talk about no lousy ingrate *ballplayer*," she snarled. And I do mean snarled.

My first thought after she cut me off again was that I'd hit a raw nerve. My second was the realization that I had a good to excellent idea what—or who—was at its root. My third was that if I was right, it would answer quite a few questions that had been puzzling me, and open the floodgates to a tidal rush of entirely new ones.

"Okay," I said. "It seems to me we're both over-due for a break. I want to go out and clear my head before diving back into these boxes."

"You mean go suck on a cigarette?"

"That might be an integral part of the head-clearing process, yes," I said. "Why do you ask?"

Thomasina shrugged a bit less mightily than before. "You want to keep puffin' away, it's your affair. But I'd rather you ease up on the smokes and stay healthy. With Royce Ramsey and his double-dealin' sidekick Liarson circlin' for the kill, all of us here need to stick around to fight them off."

I looked at her. Was that concern I'd detected in her voice? If so, I was sure it was only because my sticking around, as she put it, was—for the present—tied to the deli's survival. Still, you had to start somewhere. Who knows? Should the day ever arrive when Thom could stomach me more than a platter of spoiled herring, it was possible I'd reflect on that moment with intense fondness.

Before I got too weepy at the notion, however, I asked her to bring me the evening's dinner totals. "Let's keep up our pre- and post-Buster tragedy business comparisons," I said. "I want to see how we do tonight without the Silver Foxes. But we'll need a week or two's worth of register receipts to know how we're trending."

Thom grunted. "Princess, we get through supper without any more customers dropping dead, it'll be a real positive trend in my book," she said, turning toward the door.

That was Thomasina Jackson for you, a full-size portion of joy and moral support.

I listened to her clomp downstairs, waiting till I was fairly sure she'd left the kitchen so I wouldn't run into her on my way out. Then I grabbed my cigarettes off the desk, followed her to the bottom landing, and dashed into the alley to light up, my accumulated stress dissipating in a cloud of tobacco smoke. Well, almost dissipating, temporarily, I should qualify.

Not that anyone was taking notes.

# Chapter Eleven

Saturday's dinner numbers were crappy. I know, I know, there isn't much Southern decorum in that assessment. But it's what my literature professor in college called *le mot juste*—the absolute, perfect word. And considering our take, it was actually a mild way of putting things.

The receipts for the night came to eighteen hundred dollars. That corresponded to sixty diners, plus or minus a few, since some customers will split a single a la carte meal between them. According to Thom, an average Saturday night's total was four thousand dollars from roughly a hundred fifty people.

I didn't need a Cray computer to see that business had declined by more than half on what's normally the busiest dining-out evening of the week. Add to it that this was June, and Main Street was hopping with summer nightlife, and the shortfall became discouraging *and* crappy.

No shocker, then, that by closing time, my wait

staff was as down as the contents of my cash drawer. Servers rely on tips to boost their income, and Saturday night is their big piñata. When they clear about a hundred dollars each in gratuities, they leave with smiles all around. The fifty dollars each of the servers took in made them look sad.

I guess if I'd had to pick a low point, it would have been watching A.J. slouch out the door after telling me she was—shudder—heading straight home to bed. It wasn't just that she'd canceled a date with her loverboy cop, though that did have something to do with it. But when you put Saturday night, A.J., and a mattress together, and the upshot was sleep rather than scandal, you knew the universe was showing serious cracks.

Our kitchen closed at eleven o'clock, and the last of the dining parties left at midnight. By twelve-thirty, my entire staff had called it quits—and that included Thom, who always stayed longer than everyone else to tidy up. With plenty of anxiety to work off, I decided to stick around my office and take care of some odds and ends.

It was about an hour before fatigue caught up with me. I'd looked over the full day's receipts, laid out their totals on a computer spreadsheet for future reference, then spent a little while unboxing and sorting out more of Murray's files. Having made some progress on that front, and with my cluster yawns increasing in frequency, I finally packed it in around two o'clock, slinging my purse over my shoulder and heading downstairs to the kitchen.

My Kizashi was out back in the deli's parking lot, and the alley running between the deli and the C&W hootenanny joint next door led straight into it. But while I'd meant to turn out the entrance to the immediate right of the stairs, I found myself pausing there at their foot a minute. I'd managed to skip eating anything besides chocolate amid the day's nonstop activity and commotion, and was a little hungry . . . okay, got me, make that starved enough to almost consider nibbling Crispy the Hog's ears to their nubs. That is, if the police hadn't carried them off along with Crispy.

The problem—besides my fridge being bare at home—was that the soonest I'd get back to Antioch would be about two-thirty, a quarter to three in the morning, and snacking on anything too heavy before I hit the sheets would invite vagrant pounds to call my thighs their own. That left out chocolate in any form, since I was genetically incapable of eating it in moderation. On the flip side, Newt had baked his Johnny Cashew pie as our house special dessert. Was a slice . . . no, a *sliver* . . . of pie and a cold glass of milk before bedtime such a degenerate sin? I needed a smile. I was in fact suffering from a smile deficit. If I wanted, I could make up for the invasion of fat cals with frowning abstinence from goodies on Sunday.

I turned away from the door into the kitchen. The ceiling fluorescents were off, but Newt had left a small light on over the range knowing I'd planned to stick around my office after everyone else cleared out. Though that light didn't do much to relieve the dimness, it only took seconds for my vision to adjust as I went toward the walk-in refrigerator.

Halfway there, I sniffed some leftover cholent, then saw it simmering on a counter to my right. Newt used an enormous slow cooker with a clay inner pot for making it, my uncle having had the insert handcrafted so he could reproduce the ancient European method of preparation, which had used clay pottery that would be buried in cooking pits or placed in baking ovens overnight. Pausing again, this time at the counter by the slow cooker, I eyed the cholent a minute and realized I'd never gotten my chance to sample it that afternoon.

This time, I had nothing to distract me. Actually, this time it *was* the distraction. I lifted the cooker's lid, reached for a wooden tasting spoon, and tried a mouthful.

*"Mmm,"* I said aloud. Uncle Murray's secret recipe called for a squirt of natural honey and smidgens of dried chipotle and cumin, giving his stew the mildest peppery-sweet tang. I closed my eyes in delight, savoring its rich, mingled flavors as they overspread my tongue. *"Mmm-mmm-mmmmm—"*

I was cooing away like that—like a contented pigeon over a pile of bread crumbs, in other words—when a crash from out in the restaurant gave me a sudden start. My hand jerking involuntarily, I hit my upper lip with the wooden spoon, splattering tiny droplets of cholent up into my nose.

I spun my head toward the double doors, the chilies in the stew instantly tickling my sinuses to bring about a hard, uncontrollable sneeze. I blinked as another sneeze came on, reflexively pinching my irritated nostrils to stifle it even while trying to peer out the glass door panels into the dining room. But I went zero for two, as my night crawler of an ex used to say. That second sneeze exploded from me before I could stop it, squirting tears from my eyes and blurring my vision—not that I could have seen into the darkness on the other side of the panels anyway. Still, it didn't help matters.

Sniffling, my eyes watery, I hurried out to investigate the noise, pushing through the double doors into the restaurant, reaching over to flip the light switches on the wall next to the doors.

As the overheads came on, and the dining room brightened, and another aggravating sneeze almost bowled me over backward, I saw that the cause of my cholent-in-nose reaction was nothing more than a couple of chairs that had fallen from a table-top. Every night before closing, we flipped them upside down onto the tables as we cleaned and swept the place, so I guessed one must have been a little unbalanced and tipped over the edge to the floor, knocking the one beside it down too.

Done with my sneezing fit, I went over and picked up the chairs, setting them back onto the table. Then I gave the dining room a perfunctory look, shut the lights back off, and returned to the kitchen and my quest for some cashew pie.

The walk-in cooler was a large eight-foot square with shiny stainless steel-plate door and walls. A dial thermometer in front—its casing was also steel—said it was thirty-five degrees Fahrenheit inside the unit, but I would have known it was plenty cold without so much as glancing at it. Pulling open the door, I was hit by a blast of refrigerated air that instantly made me shiver.

I entered the lighted interior, scanned the tiers of recessed floor-to-ceiling shelves. The meat and poultry was on the right, the produce on the left, our homemade desserts and dairy goods in back facing the open door. There were cartons of soft drinks, milk crates, and other supplies along the sides of the unit, along with a hand truck for carting them around. Since the cops had dutifully carried off many of our perishables the night before, the cooler was relatively bare . . . aside from the shelves of dessert. As they did at the start of every weekend, Newt and his two-man kitchen crew had whipped up a storm of bakery items that morning, and just the pleasure of seeing them all there together might have been worth having my teeth chatter.

I saw cheesecakes, pound cakes, apple cake, carrot cake, and, naturally, several varieties of chocolate cake, Mississippi Mud and Brooklyn Blackout being high on my list of heavenly faves. I saw custards, cobblers, strudels, parfaits, fresh-fruit Jell-O salads, cream tarts, and cookies. I saw pies galore—one does not run a restaurant in the South without featuring a large selection of pies. There was lemon meringue, key lime, apple, blueberry, strawberry, peach, sweet potato, pumpkin, pecan . . . and my non-chocolate dessert amour du jour, the Johnny Cashew.

I zoned in on it, and was thinking I'd take a few extra slices for Cazzie and the kids in case they came over or Caz invited me over to their place to watch a movie or something. Then it struck me that I really needed more than a single slice of pie for myself—at least two anyway—not because I was greedy, oh no, but so as to be a giving and considerate neighbor, since it was bound to make Caz and her little darlings feel awkward if I finished my slice before they ate theirs and then sat around looking envious and needy while they stuffed their faces. Finally, I decided it only made sense to take the whole pie home. My vice . . . ah, *slice* count was already up to five or six after all. Five or six slices minimum, and what if Jimmy and Cole asked for second helpings? I had to be ready, and that would barely leave enough cashew pie at the restaurant to be called a legitimate pie. Say, for example, a bunch of customers asked for slices at the same time. And say we could only fill some of their orders. Nothing made a diner more crotchety than being the odd man out.

Okay, then, it was settled. The whole pie it would be. I'd leave a note for Newt to bake a fresh one in the morning. He wouldn't mind. In fact, he'd probably be flattered to know the Johnny Cashew was such a huge hit with me.

I would remember being about to step deeper into the refrigerator and pull out the shelf that was loaded up with pies. I'd also remember my thoughts about Newt. But these things would be *all* I remembered clearly for a while except for the hard, violent shove from behind that knocked me forward off my feet and into the wall of desserts. After that, I would have vaguer recollections of my forehead crunching against the front edge of a metal shelf with tremendous force, and maybe of bouncing backward to hit the floor of the refrigerator on my side, landing on my wrist as it twisted under me at a bad angle.

And there was one other memory that would return to me in time. Although I guess you could count it as two.

I would recall the sound of the walk-in's door slamming shut behind me and my abrupt plunge into darkness.

And finally . . .

Put the words "out" and "cold" side by side and you wind up with "out cold," which very accurately described how I lay sprawled at the rear of the refrigerator, shut away inside its thick steel walls with not a soul to help me as I grew colder and colder by the second.

# Chapter Twelve

I was cold longer than I was out. Luckily, I would discover.

I didn't know how long I'd lain unconscious on the floor of the refrigerator before my eyes fuzzily opened in the darkness. Nor did I know what hit me at first. Then I realized it was my head that had done the actual hitting when it clunked against a metal pullout shelf. And then I remembered that I'd been pushed into the shelf . . . which to me was practically the same as being hit.

I won't claim I preferred being the *hittee* to the hitter. True, it would have been ignominious to have tripped over my own feet while snatching a nosh. True too, I had already damaged my ego by having somehow managed to run Uncle Murray's legacy as a restaurant owner onto the rocks in no time flat. Nobody enjoys being a loser, and feeling like a gold-medal klutz was adding insult to injury.

But never mind my bruised ego. I knew the throbbing bruise on my *forehead* hadn't resulted from an accident. Somebody had been lurking in the deli after it closed, waiting to attack me after everyone else left. And that was a scary thought. Scarier when I remembered the refrigerator door slamming shut with a decisive bang. Scarier still because my teeth were chattering and my skin was goose-bumpy from the cold and everything around me was pitch black.

And the scariness didn't exactly end there.

As I rolled from my side onto my stomach, bracing myself on both hands so I could stand up, I felt a bolt of pain shoot through my right wrist. Wincing, I remembered falling on top of it, shifted my weight onto my left hand, and then pushed to my feet—only to lose my balance and go teetering to the extreme right.

Fortunately, I was able to steady myself before I went down in a heap. But I'd realized my right shoe was gone. I had worn three-inch dress wedges to work, and one of them must have flown off my foot when the pusher hit me, or hitter pushed me, take your pick. It had left me standing at a tilt, the bottom of my shoeless foot covered only in thin nylon hose and freezing on the grilled metal floor.

I crouched and blindly felt around for the shoe. No go. That stunk, and if I kicked off my other shoe to even my balance, I'd have not one but a pair of frigid feet. My only real option was to hobble around in the dark.

And then there was my wrist. Not to be surpassed, it had given me sharp twinges as I'd fumbled for the lost wedge. Whatever was wrong with it, I had a sneaking suspicion the problem wasn't altogether minor. I gently checked it out, pressing it with the fingers of my left hand. Ouuuch. It was tender and swollen to the touch.

*Great going, Gwen. And thank you, wrist, for getting twisted. Thank you too, grilled metal floor, for being so hard.*

I sighed. It felt like ice water shooting down my throat. My mouth shut . . . but not before my lungs seemed to fill with frost. Okay, I thought. First rule of thumb, no sighing inside a refrigerator unless I wanted an instant upper respiratory infection. Second, if I was going to talk to myself, I might as well offer constructive advice. And babbling to the floor—or scolding my appendages, for that matter— was probably a waste of time.

"I need to get out of here," I said aloud. "Find the door and get out."

There. Now that sounded like a plan. The trouble was that I'd have to feel my way around the sides of the unit in the dark. And without coming to a premature conclusion, I worried that my predicament might prove a little thornier than simply *finding* the door. If its slamming behind me hadn't sounded like a loud and clear mission statement, I did not know what would . . . and I suspected opening it might be another story. But since my goal was to get out of the refrigerator before I turned into a chilled leftover, I had to stay positive.

Then I realized something—my purse was still hanging over my shoulder. You'd have thought I'd have lost it when I was bowled over, but nice little purse that it was, it had stuck with me.

I patted it like a well-behaved dog, opened the zipper, and reached inside. My cell phone was in its pouch and I figured calling out for help was worth a try. But the refrigerator's insulated steel walls were over four inches thick, making it a long shot that I'd get a signal.

As expected, the cell was dead. I was okay with it, though. I already had another idea.

Returning the cell to its pouch, I reached into the purse's main compartment and got out my cigarette lighter. It was a lacquered Coco Chanel butane that I'd bought back in New York at a fancy little chocolate stand upstairs in Bloomingdale's. There had been a handful of vintage items in a glass case, the lighter among them, and I'd swung a good deal for it after buying a fifty-dollar box of truffles. Of course, my budget had gotten killed on the pricey truffles . . . but we won't go there.

I found the lighter, thumbed the starter button, and a small orange flame sprouted up. Then—*presto!* Its glow revealed the refrigerator door to my right, and then my missing wedge in a corner under the meat and poultry shelves. There'd be no need to do any groping after all.

The little flame held out in front of me, I tottered over to the shoe, slid my foot into it, and rushed over to the door. There was a manual light switch beside it, and I flipped it on to override the automatic cutoff. As brightness filled the space around me, I blinked a few times, dropped the lighter back into my purse, and pushed on the door handle.

The door didn't open.

I pushed again, harder, and pretended not to notice the vapor puffing from my mouth.

It wouldn't budge.

I couldn't have said I was surprised. Disheartened, frightened, and increasingly desperate, sure. But the real surprise would have been if the door opened. Whoever pushed me had obviously meant business. Something was jamming it shut from the outside.

*So now what?*

I figured I could scream and bawl for starters. Except there was nobody around to hear me, and hysterics wouldn't make the door open on its own. All it would do, in fact, was exhaust me . . . and the oxygen in the unit.

On the other hand, the cold had gotten so unbearable, my teeth were rattling like maracas. I couldn't take much more of it. And I was not about to rumba.

"C'mon," I whispered to myself. "Can we please have some inspiration here?"

I reached into my purse for a cigarette. Though I had no intention of lighting up, it would assuage my oral fixation and maybe let me calm down enough to think.

I poked it into my mouth. And thought. I couldn't open the door. I also couldn't stay where I was all night without hypothermia setting in. My only way out was to get help to come. But that wouldn't be as easy as getting my cigarette lighter out of my purse. How . . . ?

My forehead might have creased. I wasn't positive because the cold had completely numbed it. Like my lips, cheeks, and fingertips. But I had a habit of wrinkling my brow when brainstorms struck.

I looked up at the refrigerator's ceiling panel and

carefully examined it. Besides the light fixture, it was featureless except for two rows of nozzles angling downward from pipes along the left and right sides of the unit.

I had a tendency to think of the refrigerator as a room. That was wrong, though. What it was, was a giant appliance. And the pipe and nozzle assemblies were part of the appliance's fire-suppression system. When I inherited the restaurant, our insurance agent had informed me that it had been installed quite a while back and used a chemical powder to extinguish flames. She had explained that modern systems used a more efficient liquid agent, and had offered to significantly lower my premiums if I replaced the old one. I'd had no beef with the recommendation, but had found the new systems pricey and decided to hold off on the switch until the deli started bringing in some revenue.

My eyes traced the pipes along their path below the welded seams where the walls met the ceiling. Searching, searching—and then they stopped.

"There," I said. "There you are."

I'd located the mechanism that would trigger the system in the event of a fire . . . two metal links held together by a strip of red plastic. As our insurance agent had explained it, if the plastic was exposed to high heat, the fusible links would separate and initiate an automatic process that released the chemical powder. But that wasn't all. There were sensors—microswitches, the agent had called them—that would activate a fire alarm and shut down the cold-air blowers, exhaust fans, and other electrical equipment that might cause the flames to spread.

"Okeydoke." My head was craned so far back that the Pall Mall I'd lipped was pointing almost straight upward. "Now . . . how'm I supposed to reach you?"

*Okeydoke? How'm?* Where had they come from? Next thing I knew, I'd be *ya'alling.*

But never mind that, I thought. On a good day, when my posture wasn't too slouchy, I stood about five-four. That would make me five-seven with my wedges on—a stable, unwobbly height on both sides now that I'd recovered my right shoe. It left over two feet between the top of my head and the ceiling, and the fire-suppression system's piping hung a few inches *below* the ceiling.

I moved to where I'd spotted the fusible link above some cartons of soda near the produce shelves, carefully stepped up onto one, and reached for the link with my good hand. My fingertips came a little short of touching it. Standing on my toes wasn't an option in the wedges—I'd just rock forward in them and take another spill. So what then?

I looked around for something to boost me up, my eyes landing on the hand truck that I'd spotted before. It was on the opposite side of the refrigerator by the milk crates, and though it didn't stand very high, there were three metal crossbars running across the frame kind of like rungs on a ladder. If I could wheel it over and climb up onto the middle rung . . . it might give me the boost I needed.

I hurried to the hand truck, rolled it over, engaged the wheel lock, and leaned it over the soda cartons so its handle was braced against the wall. Then I pushed down on it, testing to make sure it stayed put. Finally, I got the Chanel lighter out of my purse, turned its butane control knob to its highest setting, and stepped up onto the hand truck's middle rung, gripping one side of the frame with my right hand despite the fresh cry of misery it prompted from my wrist.

Holding the lighter over my head, I clicked on the flame and it jumped up to the fusible link. Then I waited anxiously, vapor puffing from my nose and mouth in the awful refrigerator cold.

Seconds passed. The flame licked at the plastic band. I didn't have a clue how long the lighter would burn. I couldn't know whether the fire would be hot enough to melt the band. I could only hope.

Soon the lighter began to get uncomfortably warm in my grip . . . and with the flame burning so high, it was no wonder. It didn't seem to be doing much to the fuse, though, and that hardly encouraged me.

My confidence took another hit when I noticed the lighter starting to flicker a little. I had a hunch one of my question marks was about to be erased, and not as I'd wished for. Although the flame was still hot, I was growing fearful it would peter out before it melted the fuse. And would that honestly be a surprise? A cigarette lighter wasn't a torch after all.

I could feel my heart sinking like a weight. No,

it definitely wasn't a torch, I thought. It wasn't meant to sustain an intense flame. The butane canister just didn't contain enough of a charge to let it burn for an extended per—

*Keep ridin' Gwennie! Stay on the horse and keep ridin'! You know it's what I'd do!*

I resisted the impulse to snap a glance back over my shoulder. It was impossible, of course. But I could have sworn. . . .

No. I wouldn't even let myself contemplate it. I mean, come on. I did *not* believe in guardian angels, and pinning my hopes on one now would be beyond pathetic. Besides, I knew Uncle Murray. He'd have found better ways to spend his afterlife than haunting a walk-in refrigerator. This was still a Saturday night, and if anything he would be on some boozy cloud jamming with the ghostly bar band of his choice. Maybe, he'd have talked the spirits of Buck Owens and Les Paul into backing him on guitar. Possibly, he'd even charmed the shade of Tammy Wynette into a vocal duet. Among other things to follow.

Still, I'd give Uncle Murray's benevolent specter his due. Though my arm was already tired from holding the lighter steady over my head, and the flame was visibly lower than before, I would keep the lighter up to the fuse strip until it altogether petered out. What other choice was there besides quitting? And how would that do me any good?

*Definitely Tammy Wynette on vocals,* I thought, trying to take my mind off my straining, upraised arm. With apologies to Ms. Lynn and her eensie squaw mini-dress, Murray'd always had a special thing for Tammy, who would have gotten his internal fire alarms ringing as loud as the alarm I'd suddenly heard kick in somewhere around me, and—and—wait a minute . . . the *fire alarm was ringing?*

I blinked, looked up, and barely had time to register that the plastic strip had melted from the fuse mechanism's links when streams of talcy powder started gushing from the nozzles under the ceiling, billowing all around the walk-in's interior, blanketing everything in whiteness. It was as if I'd found myself in the heart of a wild, enveloping blizzard— the stuff was smothering me, getting into my eyes, my nose, my mouth, blinding and choking me even as fire bells clanged relentlessly away outside the steel-plated walls of the refrigerator.

Coughing, wheezing, I teetered on the rung of the hand truck, unable to keep my balance. I thought I heard myself scream, but might have only imagined it as I involuntarily let go of the hand cart's frame and went crashing down hard on my back, smacking into the thick drifts of powder that had overspread the shelves, carton, and floor. And speaking of the floor . . . as I sprawled there again, the dry fire suppressant covering me till I resembled one of those Pompeii people in natural history exhibits, I couldn't help but wonder about something.

In hindsight, would it have been so very awful if I'd tried to wait out the night in the fridge after all?

# Chapter Thirteen

"Gwen?" Beau McClintock said. "Are you okay?"

Crouched in the middle of the refrigerator with a large cookie sheet over my head, I peered at the detective through a haze of floating powder. He hadn't arrived alone—firefighters, uniformed police officers, and men in EMT clothing had come racing in with him as the unit's door flew open.

"Y-yeah," I sputtered. I slanted one end of the cookie sheet downward and a heap of fire suppressant spilled off. It felt as if the accumulated load had weighed a pound. "What . . . how did you . . . ?"

I let the sentence dangle, not sure what I'd meant to ask him. Or maybe it was that I didn't know which of my questions to ask first. Needless to say I was pretty out of it.

McClintock relieved me of the baking sheet and made way for an emergency services tech, who knelt in front of me and draped a blanket over my shoulders.

A big, strong guy with a shaved head and star tattoo on his neck, he started to slide two fingers under my right wrist, saw me withdraw it protectively, then noticed the swelling and carefully explored it with his fingers.

"Looks like you've got a sprain there, ma'am . . . nothing too bad," he said. "We'll get a pressure wrap around it. In the meantime, I'll use your left arm to take your pulse if that's okay."

I nodded as he went about his business, glancing at his wristwatch to measure my pulse rate.

"Appears you're alive," he said. An ophthalmoscope had appeared in his hand. "You have any pain or numbness . . . especially in your fingers, toes, lips or ears?"

"They were a little numb before," I said. "It's nothing worse than I used to feel every winter in New York."

An easy smile, and he studied my eyes through the scope. Then he rose and turned to McClintock. "Vitals are normal, no signs of shock," he said. "She's a little pale, though. Probably some mild hypothermia."

McClintock grunted and took the EMT's place crouching over me.

"Are you able to stand? There's a stretcher in the kitchen . . . the techs can bring you to the hospital, have a doctor check you out to be on the safe side."

"That's all right," I said. "I'm good."

He looked at me. "I saw you favoring that wrist a minute ago."

I shrugged, powder trickling from under my blouse sleeves. "I might have turned it the wrong way . . . it won't kill me," I said. And then remembered one of the things I'd wanted to know from him. "What was keeping the door shut? I pushed the panic bar but it didn't budge."

McClintock looked at me, taking gentle hold of my elbow. "We'll get to that in a minute," he said. "In the meantime, how about I help you up? We'll be extra careful of that wrist."

I nodded and slowly got to my feet, his hand bracing me. Though I wouldn't have said I was faint or dizzy, I still didn't feel quite right and was thankful for his assist.

"Ma'am, if you please, could you tell me what set off the alarm?" said one of the firemen. He was looking around the refrigerator, which I realized had gotten warmer inside. Probably the fire-suppression system had cut the power to the cold-air blowers. "I don't notice that anything's burned . . . other than the fuse."

"And that's all you'll see," I said, summarizing how I'd gotten stuck in the fridge, then tripped the system with my lighter. "I was afraid I'd freeze or run out of air if I couldn't get out."

"Good thinking too," said the EMT who'd examined me. "The temperature would have been almost freezing in here before things shut down . . . I've seen people suffer from severe exposure in warmer conditions."

So much for my second thoughts about what I'd done to raise a commotion. I drew the ends of the blanket together over my shoulders, wanting to get back to the question I'd asked McClintock a moment ago. "Detective—"

"Beau," he reminded me.

"Beau," I said. "Someone snuck up on me from

behind . . . pushed me hard enough to knock me out. Whoever did it . . . do you think . . . that is . . . in your opinion, was the person trying to . . . ?"

The words I was shooting for were *kill me.* But I couldn't get them to leave my mouth.

McClintock's eyes settled on my face. "When the fire alarm was reported, I headed over with a few men right away . . . and with headquarters being so close, we were at the scene before the firemen and EMS ambulance," he said. "We broke the lock on the side door, came through the kitchen, and saw a chair wedged against the refrigerator's outer door handle."

I looked back at him. My vision was a little blurry, and I felt granules of the fire suppression chemical in my eyes and tear ducts. "Just before I walked into the refrigerator, I heard a loud noise from the restaurant," I said. "I went to see what caused it and found a couple of chairs knocked over on the floor."

"You didn't find it suspicious?"

"No," I said. "It seemed to me that they fell off a table. We set them there, you know—"

"When you're doing your cleanup."

"Exactly," I said. "Sometimes people are in too much of a hurry to go home and get careless."

"So you didn't consider it unusual."

"Right."

I shook my head, pushed a stray lock of hair from my face. It was gritty with powder. "If one's a little unbalanced, it can tip over and have a domino effect. I've gotten here in the morning and found three, four chairs on the floor. That's almost a whole table's worth."

McClintock rubbed a fingertip over his cheek, his gaze holding on me. I heard his nail scrape a light stubble of beard. "Gwen, do you have any idea who might want to hurt you?"

I shook my head again.

"There've been no incidents? With customers? Staff members?"

"No," I said. "Unless you want to count what happened to Buster Sergeant."

He scratched his cheek some more. "The restaurant's doors were locked, right?"

I nodded. "You told me you had to break in the side door. And I'm the one who let Thomasina out the front entrance. That takes care of both."

"Then it seems probable that whoever attacked you would've been hiding here," McClintock said. "Waiting for you to leave your office."

I hadn't gotten that far in processing what had occurred, but it did make sense from one perspective. "I guess," I said. "This isn't a huge restaurant, though. It's hard to come up with places where somebody could stay out of sight the whole time we were closing."

McClintock seemed to let his mind hang on that a moment. Then, after a silence, he said, "So I don't forget to ask . . . what time was it when you heard the noise?"

"Maybe two o'clock," I said. "Could've been a little afterward."

McClintock looked thoughtful.

As he started asking another question, I abruptly

realized that I didn't know what time it was and checked my watch. It was after four in the morning. Incredibly—or incredibly to *me*—I'd been stuck in the refrigerator for a couple of hours.

". . . by the time you heard them," McClintock said.

I looked at him. My attention had momentarily drifted. "Excuse me? I hope I don't seem too scatterbrained . . . but I must've missed something."

"Not to worry, it's been some weekend around here." He paused. "You'd said it was about two A.M. when you heard those chairs crash down. And that made me wonder if you always stick around that late."

"No," I said. "I was straightening up my office . . . my uncle left it in a state most of us would call chaotic."

McClintock nodded, a thin smile gradually spreading across his lips. "I'm not surprised," he said.

That smile . . . I couldn't interpret it. But I did recall the weird vibe I'd detected between him and Thomasina after the Buster Sergeant catastrophe, and then remembered Thomasina's angry ballplayer comment from earlier in the night. Well, *last* night now.

"Beau," I said, "did you know my uncle well?"

He appeared surprised by the question. "Well enough," he said. "Why do you ask?"

"Just curious," I said without elaboration. I'd picked up on some hesitation from him, and it convinced me that wasn't the right time to share my reasons. Meanwhile, the firemen and emergency workers had begun filing out of the refrigerator and kitchen, making me want to get going myself. "Anyway . . . if it's okay with you, I'd like to head on home."

McClintock studied my features again. "I'll need a full statement from you for my report . . . but we can do that at my office tomorrow afternoon," he said. "Meanwhile, you sure you're feeling up to the drive?"

"I'm a little sluggish," I said. "But I'll be okay with it once those techs give me the pressure bandage."

"And there's somebody to give you a hand if you need it?"

"I can always call my neighbor Cazzie," I said. "We have adjoining condos."

"You live alone?"

"Unless you count Southpaw and Mr. Wiggles."

He looked at me.

"My two cats," I said.

McClintock grunted. "I'd be happy to give you a lift, Gwen," he said. "As a precaution."

"Thanks but no thanks," I said. "Really. It's a short trip up to Antioch."

He went on looking at me without seeming to be persuaded. "How about I tag along behind you in my car? This way we can be positive you get home safe."

I sighed. Bearing in mind what had gone on at the restaurant over the last couple of days, I strongly doubted his persistent concern was limited to my driving. I also couldn't find a reason to quarrel with it.

"Sure," I said finally. "As long as you won't tail-gate."

McClintock's smile was very quick this time. "You've got a deal," he said.

# Chapter Fourteen

Between my getting home in the fuzzy hours between Saturday and Sunday and returning to the restaurant, it was a lightning-fast turnaround.

After waving good night to McClintock—who chivalrously pulled in front of the condo and waited there for me to park the car, then walk inside from the attached garage and turn the lights on—I had enough time left over to feed the kitties, pop a few Tylenol to quiet my achy wrist, shower the chemical dust out of my hair (since I hopefully wouldn't have to worry about it bursting into flames otherwise), and catch about three hours' sleep before getting up at seven A.M. to phone Thomasina and Newt and throw them into separate but equal panics with my account of my little adventure in Fridge-land.

And you think that was an earful to hear, imagine having to live it.

I had no real clue if we'd be able to swing our regular Sunday noon brunch as I staggered blearily back to my car amid chimney puffs of cigarette smoke, a dull throb in my wrist and paper cup of black coffee in hand. I was determined to give it a shot, though. Although the refrigerated goods had been ruined, we had everything that was out front in the prepared food and unrefrigerated dessert cases, all the cured meats hanging *behind* the cases, and whatever was in the freezer. My inclination was to open the doors for business, wing it with whatever dishes we could serve, and hope for the best.

This would be contingent on how Thomasina and Newt weighed in once we got together, however. I was very matter-of-fact about my professional strengths and weaknesses, and wasn't ashamed to fess up to being the least experienced of the three of us. They'd know best what we could swing in a crisis.

As I drove past the alley between the restaurant and Trudy's Country and Blues Club at ten-thirty, I saw a locksmith working on the side door, and automatically handed it to Thom for rustling him out of bed . . . no small feat on a Sunday morning in Nashville. Whatever coercive tactics she'd used—physical violence, blackmail, waterboarding, or threatening to drag him to one of her church functions—I figured she'd spared no effort imposing her will on the poor guy. I was also hoping it might be a sign that Thom shared my determination to serve brunch to anyone that showed up with a need to eat.

Leaving the Kizashi in its usual spot behind the restaurant, I came around to the front entrance with a semi-optimistic feeling in my heart, a near bounce in my stride, and maybe a flicker of extra glowiness at the tip of my second smoke of the young morn. My wrist wasn't even throbbing too badly, thanks to my washing down another dose of Tylenol with the dregs of my coffee. Life might not be good, but I would embrace more or less acceptable for now.

Alas, all things must pass, *hare hare*. With apologies to George Harrison. I'd obviously never met Royce Ramsey or his slime-acious legal flunky . . . er, dutiful counselor-at-law . . . Cyrus Liarson in the flesh. But some people exude a certain unique eau de creep, and I pinned those two stinkers the second I looked through the door and saw them slinking around Thom's hostess station.

The tall, lean man I took to be Ramsey was wearing a Stetson Panama hat with a leather band and feather, exactly like the kind Thom described from when he'd stopped by the deli after my uncle's funeral. No white suit this time, but a tan sport coat that shouted high-end Canali to me, a tieless white shirt tucked into his blue jeans, and high-heeled, pointy-toed Western boots. His eyes were covered by dark aviator glasses, and his hair seemed very close to buzz cut under the hat. I assumed he was going for the Rugged Intimidator look, although Cattleman Entrepreneur was a straightforward possibility.

Liarson, meanwhile, was a short, pudgy man of average height with a receding hairline, small eyes, pencil mustache, and peculiarly undershot chin. I guessed his plain navy blue suit was supposed to convey Can-Do Professional, but his tasseled loafers with their punched-hole pattern instantly got me stuck on Grown Up Buster Brown. Though he'd left his old-fashioned sailor hat, bowtie, and loyal companion Tige home that morning, I did notice a brown leather portfolio-style briefcase tucked nattily under his arm.

I rolled my eyes skyward. Was it okay to pray for people to so completely vanish from existence that they didn't even leave behind sub-molecular trace particles? I didn't know. Not any more than I knew if a Jewish girl could pray on Sunday *period,* since it might mistakenly route the request through the wrong channels and muck up the heavenly works.

This was really and truly the last thing I'd needed. I had braced for a rough day. I'd been prepared to spend part of it coming to grips with the knowledge that some skulker had lingered in the restaurant after closing the night before, by all appearances planning to kill me. I'd understood I would need to assess the financial hit that would stem from having the contents of our walk-in refrigerator rendered inedible by chemical powder. And I was all too aware that I might have to cast a decisive vote on whether we opened for brunch or kept our doors closed to business—knowing full well the latter could only send a terrible message to patrons whose confidence in us was already shaky at best.

Still, I hadn't been ready to dosey-do with Royce and Liarson. Seeing them in the deli was almost enough to make my untameably curly lid flip on arrival . . . which was why I decided to go into full denial mode and pretend they weren't there as Thom came around her podium to let me in.

"Good mornin', Nash," she said, opening the door. And jabbed her chin at the unwelcome visitors. "Leastways, I'm *wishing* for a good one. Poor as the outlook might be, it's best to stay on the sunny side."

I gave Thomasina a cheerful look, flicked my cigarette butt to the sidewalk, crushed it out with the bottom of my shoe, then picked it up so I could dispose of it inside. "I'm heading upstairs . . . is everything under control here?"

"There ain't a nuisance on earth I can't handle."

"All right then." I started past the two men. "I'll be in my office."

"Ms. Silver, if we may speak for a moment." The guy I had assumed was Liarson moved in front of me to block the aisle. "I'd like to introduce you to my client, Mr. Ramsey. I contacted him after my excellent telephone conversation with you was cut short yesterday . . . I presume because of trouble on the line. To avoid further lapses in communications, we concluded it would be useful to take the initiative and—"

"Thom, something seems to be making objectionable noises." I paused, turned to face her. "Have you noticed?"

"Buzzards," she said.

"Really?"

Thom nodded. "That's what I meant by a nuisance. I saw this pair hoverin' around when I drove up and recognized the one with that straw nest on its head." She gestured at Ramsey and Liarson. "This pair's the ugliest in creation . . . you know the birds mate for life, right?"

"No," I said. "But I see how it could be true."

"One sinks its claws into another, what're the odds it'll get lucky a second time? So they stay together. Repugnant as they are, even buzzards find it hard lovin' other buzzards."

"That makes absolute sense," I said. "Listen, I want to meet with you and Newt. Let's make it in about ten minutes . . ."

Ramsey abruptly stepped between us. "Ms. Silver, I'd hoped for *five* minutes of your time when I came on down from my ranch this morning." he said. "If we could sit down and chat privately at one of your tables, I don't even reckon it would delay your meeting."

I craned my head, looking around him at Thom. "Those vultures—"

"Buzzards."

"Right, sorry, I get my carrion eaters confused," I said. "Anyway, I'm afraid those two revolting scavengers might've flapped in the door."

"That's the case, we'll want to have one of the boys chase them out with a broom."

"You think?"

"Either a broom or a water hose to wash away the filth they're bound to have carried in with them . . ."

"There's no call for this verbal abuse," Liarson objected, turning his attention my way. He'd positioned himself alongside Ramsey so they both had their backs to Thom now. "My client's driven over fifty miles to see you on a Sunday morning, and asks only that you show the basic courtesy of hearing out his offer—"

"All right, that's it! Never mind *her,* you stink-mouthed, roadkill-pickin', snake-gut-suckin' low-life." Thom took a giant step away from her podium and came around to where I stood facing the men, parking her broad form next to me, jabbing her finger across the aisle in their direction. "You want to hear real insults, go ahead and show me your backsides again. Because I hate rudeness and ain't nowhere near warmed up yet."

I resisted the urge to glance over my shoulder at Thom. My God, were we *bonding*?

Meanwhile, Ramsey was giving her a long, lingering look of his own. It seemed to show disdain and mild astonishment before he regained his poise. "Come, Ms. Silver, why not give yourself a chance to evaluate my proposal? It's surely in your best interest."

I looked at him. "That so?" I said, figuring it was my turn to follow Thom's lead and plague his existence. "How can you presume to know *what's* in my interest?"

"Because I am a real-estate developer," Ramsey said. "My success depends on evaluating whole neighborhoods to find out how they might be bettered. How they might *grow.* And I've learned to view every business as a community in miniature."

"Great speech if you decide to run for office," I said. "But it's got nothing to do with me."

Ramsey's eyes bore in on mine. "With utmost

respect, I would suggest it has everything to do with you," he said. "May I be frank, Ms. Silver?"

I couldn't have explained why it annoyed me that he kept repeating my name. But it did. "Be my guest," I said. "Just don't think I'm giving you all day."

He lifted his straw hat off his head, brought it down in front of him with both hands, and held its brim flatly over his heart. The picture of bogus sincerity. "We can't pretend your delicatessen isn't struggling right now. It's no shame. When I was a young boy, I learned that even a star goes through a natural life cycle. It's born. It shines. It might even become the hottest, most brilliant thing in the sky . . . but sooner or later, it fades," he said. "Restaurants are akin to that. Some dining places last longer than others, but not even the most popular ones stay hot forever. Public tastes are fickle. The competition moves in and everyone has a yen to see what it offers. Before long, it's the trendy place to be. Toss in fad diets and what they call demographic shifts, meaning—"

"Look, all this is making my head spin," I said. "We were supposed to be getting to the point."

"Yes, Ms. Silver. You'll pardon my wordiness. I caught it from my dad on those glorious nights he'd build a fire under the night sky, settle me down in its light and warmth, and teach me so many other valuable life lessons."

I looked at him. Was it my imagination, or had he wordily apologized for being wordy? When he finally did stop talking, I figured it was just a buildup to an a cappella rendition of "Home on the Range."

But Ramsey didn't break into song for me. Instead, he said, "Believe it or not, Ms. Silver, I'm here to spare your deli from fading like an old star. Because it's got something even the biggest and brightest of them don't possess. And I'll give you one guess what that is."

I shrugged. "Kishka?" I said. Which, I should maybe explain, was me trying to be acerbic by naming a type of kosher sausage.

Ramsey laughed . . . a full, deep-down laugh that made his chest and shoulders heave. Finally, he removed his sunglasses, pulled a handkerchief from his inside jacket pocket, and wiped his tearing eyes.

I admit his reaction caught me off guard. New York City's supposed to be the humor capital of the world, and maybe it was once upon a time. But I'd found the mega-corporatized males who were the only types that could afford to live there anymore either had no sense of humor at all, or were too uptight to show it freely, as if giving in to a good belly laugh would put a fatal chink in their masculine sophistication. They smirked, they snarked, they talked about comedy being savvy and smart. But it had been a while since I'd seen a man laugh as openly or heartily as Royce Ramsey.

Not that I was too pleased with my reaction to *him*. Joking with the Enemy—nice going, Gwen.

When he was finally through chuckling and dabbing his eyes, Ramsey neatly folded his hankie and returned it to his jacket, leaving his shades off. "I enjoyed that, I truly did," he said. "But, you know, much as I appreciate sausage made from beef intestines—especially if it's got schmaltz in the mix instead of some low-fat veggie substitute—I can't say it's the difference maker I had in mind."

Okaaay. So he not only knew about kishka, he was a kishka connoisseur. "You told me I only had one guess."

"Fair enough," Ramsey said. "The quality your deli's got that stars *don't* is adaptability, Ms. Silver. That's because it's run by people. And what people have over everything else is the capacity to change."

I looked at him. "You're losing me again," I said. "What's your wanting to buy this place, have to do with the sun, moon, and stars?"

Liarson held up his briefcase and wiggled it in my eyes. "I've brought some material that should answer your question," he said. "If we could move to a table . . . ?"

"No chance!" Thom grunted. "It's a health code violation lettin' buzzards into the—"

I put a mollifying hand on her arm. "We might as well hear them out."

"What for?"

"Then it's done," I said, my eyes meeting Ramsey's. "And we won't have to bother with it again."

She frowned. Ramsey smiled. I struck a middle ground and pursed my lips.

"Once is enough if an explanation's any good, Ms. Silver," he said finally.

I nodded, waved for Thomasina to lead us up the

aisle, and she took us toward a booth at the rear with a floor-shaking stomp in her step.

Oh, and before I forget—good laugher or not, I still didn't like Ramsey. Or the fact that he kept repeating my name all the time.

# Chapter Fifteen

"What you see is a proposal for the multipurpose entertainment venue we call Ramsey Land," Liarson was saying.

I half expected to hear trumpets bellow out a fanfare. "Clever handle," I said. "Did it take a whole team to brainstorm it?"

The thinnest of smiles materialized on Ramsey's mouth before he began rubbing its corners with his thumb and forefinger—as if to erase any suggestion of it.

Liarson apparently didn't share his evil leader's appreciation for repartee. "It is a *working* name," he said. "Lest you grow too amused, I would urge you to consider that Ramsey Land will be the largest construction project in downtown Nashville since the Bridgestone Arena."

"But unlike Bridgestone, it won't be some big unfriendly eyesore," Ramsey said. He spun his hat around a finger. "My facility will embrace Nashville's history. Its design elements will reflect Southern grace and charm. It will be an *attraction* in the truest sense of the word."

"Kind of like the places on Broadway you want to tear down," I said, glancing up from the picture in the brochure. "The Western Swing Inn, Stagecoach Bar, Trudy's . . . and of course Murray's Deli. To name a few."

Ramsey didn't look amused now. "You're an intelligent woman, Ms. Silver. It's admirable that you've undertaken to keep your uncle's restaurant solvent. I've shown you great respect . . . *all kinds* of respect . . . and wish you'd give some in return."

I shook my head. "Who's being disrespectful?" I said. "I just can't fathom why anyone who really cares about Downtown would bulldoze what's here and replace it with papier-mâché."

"That's a mischaracterization. Take a close look at the pictures in my brochure. At the authentic detail that's in them."

Thom scowled from the booth seat beside me. "I'll answer your question if he won't, Nash. Pure and simple, this buzzard wants to build somethin' fake that matches what he sees in the mirror. Him talk about charm? The only kind he knows is a dollar sign."

While Thom wouldn't have won any tactfulness awards, I understood her loathing of the facility Ramsey had planned. Its columns, dormers, and fancy roof moldings were too much of a good thing, bundling every classic architectural feature into an exaggerated monstrosity lifted from a Hollywood studio lot or the Vegas Strip.

Ramsey had kept watching my face. "Your manager here misreads me," he said. "I told you about the cycle of neighborhood popularity and decline. Do nothing to revitalize an area, to renew it for the future, and it will exhaust itself."

Liarson nodded his agreement. Shocker there, huh? "Our economic projections show lower Broadway trending toward the early decline phase," he said. "This might not be evident to its business owners. But statistics show it is inevitable in the coming months."

"That's idiotic," I said. The streets were packed every weekend. "The bars and clubs are jumping. And you want me to believe they only *look* like they're in good shape?"

"Perceptions aren't trustworthy indicators," Liarson said. "Mr. Ramsey's team uses sophisticated computer-modeling techniques. Cutting-edge software—"

"Buzzard shit," Thomasina said. "May the Good Lord forgive my Sunday cussin'."

Ramsey didn't say anything. Neither did anyone else. I'd never heard Thom use foul language before—Saturdays, Sundays, and weekdays included—and sat there waiting for lightning to strike.

A.J. might not have qualified as she strutted around to polish the silverware at a nearby table. But she certainly delivered enough sizzle wearing a pink stretch halter, a black ruffle miniskirt, and high-heeled spaghetti-strap shoes, with a butterfly tattoo in all its winged glory on her ankle.

Seated across from me in the booth, Liarson swiveled his head around to watch her, his beady little eyes dropping to her stockingless, shiksa-shapely legs.

"Mister, you find me wipin' a fork with a napkin so interesting, you're welcome to come over and help," she said. "If not, you might want to clean the crud from your weddin' band instead."

Talk about going from mesmerized to mortified in a heartbeat, Liarson's cheeks flushed red as he and everyone else in our booth glanced down at his left hand. I hadn't noticed the ring before. There was no crud that I could see, but it was possible A.J. had sharper receptors.

"I fail to understand your refusal to consider my client's buyout." Liarson had shifted his attention back to me. Give him credit for a quick rebound, although I wasn't sure I liked being the *safe* one. "We've put together a generous, comprehensive package that relieves you of ownership and overheads, but affords a great many incentives. You will stay on as a minor shareholder, titular manager, and spokesperson—"

"A shill, in other words."

"Your characterization," Liarson said. "We're giving you a vital role in our promotional campaigns. You will be the face of the franchise, with your image appearing in brochures, and a contractual provision that allows for television and radio appearances. The delicatessen will occupy a central location in our dining plaza, and we will make every effort to assure the *essence* of its current motif is recreated in our modernized complex. Lastly, while Ramsey Holdings reserves the right to rename and make staff changes to the restaurant, we guarantee your employees salary-equivalent positions at Ramsey Land." His eyes swung onto Thom. "It is expected that there will be a particular requirement for ushers and ticket takers once the transition is complete."

"Ticket-takers? How *dare* you look at me when you say that, you little moth—"

I grabbed Thom's arm to stop her before she said something she'd regret. We needed her at the restaurant, not in some monastery serving out a penitential vow of silence.

"It's hard for me to believe some of the other business owners on our street went for this offer," I said, shaking my head a little as I turned toward Ramsey

"Not some," he said. "Every establishment you mentioned has committed to it."

I was quiet for a minute. Maybe that was true. Maybe Ramsey could prove it. And maybe he'd paid for their commitments by rolling truckloads of money up to their owners' doors. Without my jumping aboard, though, his project was a nonstarter. Ramsey knew it, Liarson knew it, and most importantly, I knew it. Murray's was smack dab in the middle of the block, and there was no way anybody could build around us if I held out.

"I'm sorry," I told him. "I appreciate the offer. I think it's even possible you're sincere in believing your computer predictions and theories about restaurant life cycles. But *I* don't happen to believe them. I don't intend to leave this building—"

"How has business been this weekend, Ms. Silver?" Liarson interrupted.

I gave him a dirty look, and not just because it ticked me off that *he'd* started in with the "Ms. Silver" bit. "Are you trying to imply something?"

"No," Liarson said. "I'm asking up front if your weekend grosses were deflated by the untimely death of Buster Sergeant on your karaoke stage. And while you prepare to answer . . . have you considered how people will feel about dining here when it becomes common knowledge *you* were nearly murdered on the premises last night? That you could have frozen or suffocated in your refrigerator if an alarm hadn't summoned the police and fire department to the rescue? Such a concentrated burst of negative publicity . . . well, I'm afraid it would douse even the brightest of stars in the firmament of local eateries."

I tried not to let my jaw drop. "How . . . how did you know?"

His pencil mustache started to crawl across his face. Or so I thought before I realized it was actually that he was smiling, his upper lip stretching the 'stache taut.

"I grew up in the Metro area. I have friends and family here. Went to school with people. Attended Nashville State University." Liarson stared at me, leaning forward over the table. "We're a small community, Ms. Silver. A social network. Word comes to me, word goes out. There are no secrets."

I sat there dumbstruck. A moment ago, he'd been dangling a carrot in front of me. Incentives, my face in lights, my staff manning the ticket booths of a grand new entertainment Mecca. But here was the other part. The or else. The *stick*.

I glanced over at Thom, nodding, and the two of us rose as if on cue. Then I turned to Ramsey.

"You'll have to excuse us," I said. "We have a lot to do before the deli opens for brunch."

He nodded, put on his Stetson, stood up on his side of the booth. "I hope you'll reconsider. Take some time . . . I want you to be able to think clearly and decide what's in your best interests. Once you've made your final decision, it would be my great wish that you'd feel free to contact me."

I looked at him for a moment that wound out and out, my eyes squaring on his face.

"Consider yourself contacted," I said, and walked away.

# Chapter Sixteen

"Caz," I said, "the funniest thing happened to me on the way to being strong-armed by a zillionaire and his lawyer today."

She looked at me. We were sitting on lawn chairs in the garden outside her condo, the afternoon sun beating down on our shoulders. The butterflies fluttering around her neat, colorful flower beds might have been real-life versions of the tattoo on A.J.'s ankle, but maybe that was thinking backwards.

"Dare I ask *what* happened?" Cazzie said. She reached for the pitcher on her lawn table, refilled my glass with her homemade fruit punch, then poured some into her own glass.

I reached for the punch and sipped. Caz used orange, pineapple, and pomegranate juice in her recipe, and the latter gave it a tartness I enjoyed. She had explained that the pomegranates also added antioxidants, which were supposed to be healthier for me than nicotine or caffiene . . .

though my request for formal proof was still pending.

"Okay," I said. "You ready?"

"Unless I'm supposed to be waiting for entrance music."

That sounded like a good idea to me, so I rattled the ice cubes in my glass in lieu of a drum roll. "This morning at the deli, I stopped being a gefilte fish out of water." *Ta-da*.

Her eyes widened. "You really mean it?"

"I'm dead serious," I said. "It's weird, Caz. Those men, Ramsey and Liarson, are at the deli trying to intimidate me. And honestly, they're doing a pretty decent job, walking in like they already own the place. Confident as I'm trying to act, I start to wonder how I'm supposed to stand up to this pair when no one else on Broadway seems inclined."

"That doesn't make it easy."

"No," I said. "But then all of a sudden, I realized that I'm still holding a major trump card. Without my selling them the restaurant, they're stuck. They can draw up all the plans they want, they can have a mountain of computations, they can persuade every other business owner on the street to take the money and run. The only thing they can't do while I hold out is build their downtown Oz. And knowing it made me feel. . . ."

I hesitated. Cazzie waited. I tossed in some bonus hesitation.

"Empowered?" she said.

"No," I said. *"Stubborn."*

Cazzie laughed, drank, looked at me over the

rim of her glass. "Well, there you go," she said. "One thing's for sure . . . you're sounding more like a Southerner than ever."

I sat a moment as a vagrant breeze made my hair a bigger mess than usual. It was three o'clock, and I'd driven home to feed the kitties—and truth be known, to see if Caz might be around for a brief heart-to-heart. On Sundays, the deli kept shortened hours, closing for the night at about seven P.M., and although we didn't have an official break between the morning and afternoon shifts, business had slowed enough after midday to let me slip out for a while.

"I don't want to sound gushy and oversentimental," I said. "Too much drama, you know? But I have to tell you . . . it was something else when I realized Thom had my back today."

"I can imagine it would be," she said, "since she's never been anything but at your throat."

I smiled, saluted her pithiness with a wag of my finger, and took another drink of fruit-sweetened antioxidant miracle elixir. "I've learned that a restaurant's a different animal than most businesses. The hours are never ending. It isn't like an office job where you spend most of your time alone at a desk. You're *constantly* around people, managing situations with your coworkers, your suppliers and service providers, and your customers. When you spend such an enormous chunk of your day interacting with the same group— sometimes seven days a week—you have to enjoy being around them."

"And you do, right?" Cazzie said. "That's the sense I always get from you."

"Absolutely," I said. "The guys in the kitchen are a breed of their own. They bicker constantly, but I never worry that they won't get things done. I just kind of dodge the fireworks and then stand amazed at the food that comes out of there." I smiled a little, remembering Friday night's babka controversy. "My servers are great too. Luke's like a kid brother. A.J.'s flirtatious, insatiably horny, and a dream employee. Vern, Medina, Raylene . . . they're all hardworking and conscientious. Everybody has their moments, but I've had no major problems with them."

"Bringing us to Thomasina."

"Yeah," I said. "I couldn't run the place without her. And I know how much Uncle Murray would've wanted us to get along. But instead, it's been more like we've been stuck with each other. I've invested so much of myself in the place . . . financially, emotionally, you name it . . ."

"You needed to feel you wouldn't be on your own if things got rough."

"In a nutshell," I said. "I can live with coexistence if that's the best we can do. But it's different from knowing you can depend on a person in the clutch," I said. "When A.J. and Thom wouldn't be pushed around by Royce Ramsey . . . and then were so rock solid behind me . . . that's when *I* got stubborn."

"All for one, huh?"

"Corny as it sounds," I said with a nod. "Whatever happens next, I won't fail them if I can help it."

Cazzie considered that, shooshed a fly from its erratic flight pattern around her punch glass.

"Do you have any idea what *will* happen?"

"As far as Ramsey, it depends." I shrugged. "My sense is that he's all too happy to stay in the background and have his lawyer . . ."

"What was name again?"

"Liarson, appropriately enough," I said. "Cyrus Liarson. I think he's more of a down-and-dirty hardcase than his client. A real fixer. He'll throw every trick in the book at us . . . whatever it takes to make people so wary of eating at Murray's Deli that they stay away."

"You think he'll succeed?"

"If he can keep the Buster Sergeant story going in the press, tip them off about a stalker hanging around the restaurant to attack me . . . he certainly has plenty of bullets in his gun." I sighed. "It's good for him that we're already in a financial hole. Bad for us."

"Because it puts you in a defensive position."

"Backs against the wall," I said. "We're *had* if we can't pay our bills."

Cazzie looked at me. The breeze kicked up and romped through my hair again. I brushed a few strands from my eye with my left hand, winced at a sharp twinge the sudden motion brought about in my wrist.

"Ow," Cazzie said.

"You felt my pain, huh?" I said.

"Not really, but I *did* notice it."

"It isn't so bad. I just need to avoid little things like showing off how well I can flap my arms."

She smiled, sipped her punch. "Okay if I ask a question or two about those bullets you mentioned?"

"Shoot." I grinned meekly.

"Have you found out anything new about what killed Buster Sergeant?" she said, ignoring my cleverness.

I considered how to answer. McClintock had made me promise to keep quiet about the coroner's discovery of Furadan poison in his body. Lousy as I felt about it, I couldn't tell Cazzie.

"The police want to keep it under their hats for now," I said, not quite lying.

She met my gaze. I had a hunch she'd picked up on there being more to it, but she didn't press me. "Leaving that aside," she said, "last night's incident at the restaurant has me worried. Somebody sneaked up on you from behind, pushed you with such force you were knocked unconscious, and then locked you in the refrigerator. In a district attorney's office, that falls somewhere between first-degree assault and attempted murder. I wonder . . . that is, I assume *you* must be wondering who'd have a motive?"

I sat there a minute. The fly that had buzzed around her glass alighted on my nose, momentarily made me cross-eyed, and shot away. "Caz," I said, "are you heading down the lawyerly path I think you are?"

"I'm only looking at possibilities," she said in a low voice. "Let's lay it out in the open. The notion that Royce Ramsey would want to have you killed is crazy. But no crazier than stories I've heard from friends who are criminal lawyers. The deli *is* literally the only thing standing between him and a cash-cow real-estate project. And maybe it isn't about murder. You brought up Ramsey's intimidation tactics . . ."

"You think he might have intended to throw a scare into me?"

"That *was* an effect of what happened," Cazzie said. "I know I'm scared anyway. And once the police documents become public record, the story's bound to make the newspapers, which you told me yourself would make Liarson happy."

I was imagining her reaction if I could have disclosed that Buster Sergeant's death hadn't resulted from food poisoning—at least of the accidental variety. But I couldn't afford to ponder it—she'd reminded me of something that had nearly slipped my mind altogether.

"Caz, I hate to cut this short, but I need to stop at police headquarters before heading back to the deli," I said, glancing at my watch. "Detective McClintock's still waiting for my statement—and it's getting late."

"Do tell." She put her glass down on the tray she'd brought from her condo. "Grace should have the kids home in an hour or so and there's nothing ready for them to eat."

"Sounds dangerous," I said. "I wouldn't want to leave here wondering about the safety of my cats."

She laughed as I got up, added my glass to the tray, and lifted it off the table, figuring I'd give her a hand.

"You know," I said, "I meant to bring you and the boys some Johnny Cashew pie from the restaurant."

"Seriously?"

"It was what I was getting out of the fridge last night," I said. "But whoever shoved me—and the fire extinguishers—took care of that."

She paused and looked at me midway to her back door. "Now I really want somebody punished for the deed," she said.

# Chapter Seventeen

"Okay, Gwen, I think we've covered everything." McClintock said. He picked his digital recorder up off his desk blotter. "I appreciate you giving me permission to get your statement in an audio file—it beats taking notes, and not only because I can't read the chicken scrawl that passes for my own penmanship."

I smiled from across the desk, glad to be done with the interview. Reliving my experience in the refrigeration unit hadn't been fun. Also, it was almost a quarter to five and I was impatient to return to the restaurant.

"What's the other reason?" I asked, slipping my purse strap over my shoulder. "And don't tell me it's that you like the sound of my voice."

The detective gave a small chuckle. "I'll refrain from making that admission . . . which doesn't mean it wouldn't be truthful," he said. "Frankly, it's advisable to have a recording for evidentiary purposes."

"You mean if there's an arrest?"

"And particularly at trial," he said with a nod. "Nowadays, defense attorneys scrutinize every last item of proof. I don't blame them . . . it keeps cops like me on our toes. The problem's that guilty parties have walked because the cases against them were undercut by minor inaccuracies in handwritten notes. You have to take them when there's a lot of hubbub around and the background noise might drown out people's voices—like at your restaurant Friday night. But a recording's perfect for a one-to-one here in my office. Whenever a jury can actually *listen to* a statement, it eliminates one potential stumbling block in a prosecution."

I'd stayed in my chair, thinking. "Do you feel you'll be able to catch whoever locked me in the fridge?"

"I'm not big on predictions, and that would be the last kind I'd be inclined to make," McClintock said. He shrugged. "I also don't believe much in coincidence, though. And my guess would be there's a link between Buster Sergeant's poisoning and your episode last night."

"Do you have any idea what kind of link?"

"Not yet," he said. "As of this moment, we have no suspects, no theories for what's behind these incidents, no clues . . . but we're at an early stage of the investigation.

I sat there, wondering if I should have mentioned Cazzie's suspicions about Royce Ramsey. But resentful as I was of his buyout offer, and despite my intense aversion to his stooge Liarson, neither of them had twisted my arm into accepting it—or done anything too far out of line that I knew about.

Even Liarson's having approached members of the deli's staff behind my back to entice them into getting behind the buyout was unscrupulous, but not really crooked.

It seemed a bad idea to throw his or Ramsey's name into the hat—not that I cared about creating hassles for them, but because I felt it would muddy the waters and maybe even make me look paranoid, vindictive, or both. Best to keep Cazzie's bit of speculation to myself unless or until something happened to give it credibility.

No, I'd keep that bit of supposition to myself unless something happened to give it credibility.

Satisfied I'd made the right decision, I thanked McClintock for his consideration, and was taking another shot at getting up to leave when, for the second time in as many visits to the office, I happened to notice the snapshot on the wall near his desk—a varsity baseball team in gold and orange uniforms, a younger McClintock smiling at the camera from the front row of players. That, and the baseball in its display case at one corner of his blotter.

*"Artie mentioned something about artists. Athletes too, I guess—"*

"Let's not go there."

"Huh? I—"

*"I don't want to talk about no lousy ingrate* ballplayer."

* * *

I froze halfway off my chair, staring at McClintock's photograph, recalling every word of my cheery exchange with Thomasina over Murray's penchant for helping people in need of a cash fix. How often over the past couple of days had I picked up hints that McClintock and Uncle Murray had been more than just passing acquaintances? Three, four times? Yet whenever I'd started asking about it—or broached the subject with McClintock himself, for that matter— a brick wall had gone up in front of me, as if I was raising the question at the absolute worst possible moment. . . .

"Gwen? What is it?" McClintock sprang to his feet.

"Nothing," I said. "No worries."

"You're sure? If you aren't feeling well . . ."

"Seriously," I said. "I'm fine."

We stood there looking at each other. And then it occurred to me. The two of us alone in his office, no distractions . . . maybe this was the *best* moment to ask about his relationship with my uncle. I could even use the chummy call-him-by-his-first-name, let's-get-personal ploy. Why not? He'd handed it to me gift wrapped after all.

"Beau," I said. "I've been hoping you'd tell me . . . that is, I'd like to know about you and Murray."

We must have thrashed a good, long minute to death swapping looks across his desk before he finally sat down. I followed his lead, taking it as a fair sign he wasn't about to Hail Mary me out the door.

"Guess you were looking at the photo of me,"

he said, nodding his head back at its spot on the wall behind him. "I also reckoned it caught your attention when you were here yesterday."

"Yes." I gestured at the baseball in its desktop display case. "And that too."

His head went up and down. "The colors I'm wearing in that picture belong to the University of Tennessee baseball team. The UT Vols . . . that's short for Volunteers. Fifteen years ago, I was a junior at school, a pitcher. The number-three starter in the team's rotation."

"I'm no baseball junkie . . . but isn't that a big deal?"

"It's an important role," McClintock said with a nod. "So anyway, the Chicago Cubs have a farm team over in Knoxville called the Smokies, and the Minnesota Twins have an affiliate in New Britain. And their scouts came to watch me throw, and I got drafted low by the Twins. But the Cubs wanted me even more and made a trade and picked me up."

I blinked. "Hang on. You were a Major League pitcher?"

McClintock's smile was reflective and, I thought, tinged with sadness. "Never quite . . . but I did come close," he said. "My father worked as a line-man for Middle Tennessee Electric. Mom was a secretary at a trucking firm for over thirty years. But then Pop got into an accident running cable, lost his legs, and couldn't work at all. That's with three other kids besides me to feed and clothe." He paused, shrugged. "I wasn't offered a fat signing check. Twenty-seventh-round prospects aren't bonus babies. And baseball's an iffy enough living without having to start out as anyone's financial burden. So I figured I'd have to pass on my chance to play pro ball, dream though it might've been. Graduate college, get a decent-paying regular job, and help out at home.

"That was it? You decided to stay in school?"

"Yep," McClintock said. He sighed, a long, heavy breath that seemed to come from way down around his toes. "And I would've stuck to my choice except for one kind, decent man offering to help with my family's expenses."

It sunk in all at once. "Uncle Murray," I said.

"I worked for him part-time. Started when I was a senior in high school, and went on through my three years of college."

I was shaking my head incredulously. "that's quite a long while."

"Five years in all," McClintock said. "Murray hired me as a part-time delivery boy and gofer. I used to run takeout lunches over to the music studios, keep the tips. After a bit, I started doing different odds and ends around the restaurant. Worked the register, cleaned up, and so on. Never waited tables because your uncle reserved that for full-timers."

"And when you got traded to the Cubs, he gave you a loan. . . ."

"I suppose you could call it that, even though he wouldn't ever let me repay it," McClintock said, folding his hands on the desk. "Really, it was for my family, so I could give baseball a go with a clear mind and wouldn't have to be concerned they'd fall short on paying their mortgage and bills."

I still couldn't help but be amazed by what he was telling me. "What happened after that?"

"I left school, pitched Double-A for the Smokies, and was better than anybody expected," McClintock said. "My first season in the minors, I threw the only no-hitter in team history and was going to be fast-tracked up to Triple-A." He shrugged, expelled more air through his mouth. "And then I got hurt on the mound—a shoulder injury. Last game of the year, wouldn't you know. I went through rotator cuff surgery, a year of rehab. But I never could throw the same afterward. They say shoulders are dicier than elbows, and I guess that was true for me."

I looked at him. "I'm sorry," I said. "It must've been an awful blow."

McClintock's eyes lowered to his hands for a while, then slowly returned to my face. "What happened to Pop . . . *that* was awful," he said. "Things just didn't work out as I hoped, no tragedy. I went back to school, majored in criminal law, got hired as a Metro patrolman, made my way up through the ranks. . . ."

"And here you are now," I said quietly into the silence. "A police detective."

He nodded, his gaze firmly on mine. "With my baseball mementos and the niece that Murray couldn't talk enough about."

I hesitated, wishing my cheeks hadn't felt warm all of a sudden. "There's something I still don't understand. Thomasina's attitude—the way she's so hostile to you—is it somehow connected to your not repaying the loan?"

He shook his head. "If that was it, I wouldn't be alone in this town, nor rate her meanest stares," he said. And then pinched his face in an impression of one.

I laughed. "Not bad," I said. "But it lacks the full, ornery weight of her personality."

"I don't suppose that's too easy to mimic," he said. And paused for a long moment. "Getting back to your question, Gwen . . . you do know your uncle enjoyed his gambling, right?"

"Yes," I said. "When I was little, he'd hit Aqueduct Racetrack all the time. The Big A, he called it. The track was in a New York City neighborhood called Ozone Park, maybe fifteen, twenty minutes from his house on the expressway." I chuckled. "Never mind that the beach was right in the area. One day, he'd wanted to bring me to see the thoroughbreds run there, introduce me to some of his friends in the clubhouse. Me with my hair bows and Barbie dolls. I must've been nine years old."

"I bet your parents were overjoyed."

"If I'd kept my stupid mouth shut about going with him, they wouldn't have put the kibosh on it," I said. "No kidding, though . . . being his niece was a blast. And it wasn't as if he ever stuffed one of his Cuban cigars into my mouth."

McClintock gave a thin smile. "When I was a Cubs' farmhand, Murray'd come to watch me pitch all the time. He seemed to take pride in my ability. I could count on seeing him in the stands at every home game, and sometimes on the road too."

"You're kidding."

"I swear to you, Gwen. He was like a proud

father," McClintock said. "And then I started hearing whispers about him."

"Whispers?" It took a moment for the meaning of that to sink in. "Are you saying people thought he was betting on your games?"

"The stories were that I was an investment . . . it made no difference they weren't true. Murray never broadcast that he'd fronted money to more folks than you could count, and people who didn't know him only cared about his rep as a gambler." He lifted his hands off the desk and spread them apart. "The rumors dogged me that whole season, till I finally asked Murray to stop coming to the games. There must have been a better way to handle it. If I was older, I'd have done it differently. But I was under pressure from my manager, the team owners, even some players . . . and it got to be a distraction . . . and I did what I did. And though it might've pained him to his core, I think he understood my reasons."

I looked at him, a sudden realization overspreading my features. "And Thomasina didn't."

McClintock shook his head. "No, not at all," he said. "She's as headstrong as she is loyal. And she loved him too much to be forgiving of me."

We sat in silence. I wasn't sure what else to say, and guessed he wasn't either. Then it occurred to me that we'd probably said everything necessary.

I stood up, slipping my purse over my shoulder. Then McClintock came around the desk and showed me to the door. I stood there feeling awkward for a few moments, although I wasn't quite sure why—which only made me feel more self-conscious.

If McClinctock noticed, he didn't let on. Instead, he thanked me for dropping by to give my statement, and I told him he was more than welcome, and then I left.

# Chapter Eighteen

The restaurant emptied out by seven-thirty. There hadn't been many diners, but everybody who came in got a choice of a free knish to take home and seemed pleased. The last of them, an elderly man named Earl who showed up every Sunday like clockwork, even cracked a joke that I supposed had Buster Sergeant's demise at its root.

"If I drop dead on the street from eating my free potato knish, make sure to send two of 'em home to my wife next week!" he said, stepping out onto Broadway.

I stood beside Thom as she locked the door behind him. "If he's really got a wife, how come she's never with him?" I said.

"You got to ask after hearin' a line that dumb come out of his mouth?"

I supposed she had a point. "Okay, I'm going up to the office. Is there a new key to the side door?"

She looked at me. "You don't plan on stayin' late again, do you?"

"I have more of Murray's boxes to dig through,"

I said. "I'd like to end the weekend feeling I've made some decent progress."

We stood there at the door. Behind the register, A.J. tried to act like she wasn't eavesdropping as she cashed out. It would have helped her performance if she wasn't gawking at us.

"Princess, I realize bein' a New Yorker goes along with thinkin' you're invincible," Thom said. "But how can you want to stick around this place alone after last night?"

"I can't be afraid of running my own restaurant," I said with a small shrug. "Besides, it was two in the morning when everything happened. I'll be out of here by nine o'clock tonight."

She looked uncertain. "You give any thought to figurin' out who tried to leave you packed away in the cold meats section?"

"Nice way of putting it," I said.

Thom waited, stone-faced.

I sighed. "Sure I've thought about it."

"And?"

"I don't have any answers."

"How about McClintock? He share any bright ideas with you?"

"I don't think he's reached the idea stage," I said, wanting to tell her as little as I could about my visit to his office. "Thom, why are you asking me this right now?"

She shrugged. "Maybe I ain't as smart as some hotshot detective who's gettin' paid to investigate such things. But it seems to me the person that locked you in the fridge got in and out of the restaurant on his own. And could find his way around okay."

"We don't know that it wasn't a diner who stuck around after closing," I said. "He could've hidden out and waited for me."

"Hidden where?" Thomasina said. "Ain't as if people can just squat under tables without some- one noticin' it when we sweep up."

"I haven't heard that mentioned as a possibility, Thom. Although there's a chance he could've moved around between the stairwell, restrooms . . . any number of places." I sighed. "Look, I can see why you might think it's someone with access to the deli. But even if you're right, that still leaves us with a lot of people. We've given cellar keys to our *suppliers* so they can make early deliveries. And don't tell me we ought to suspect A.J. or Luke!"

A.J. blinked offendedly behind the register. I acted oblivious.

"Those two young *fools* couldn't've harmed you if they tried," Thom said, prompting another round of eye-fluttering from our snoopy cashier. "But I don't see what's wrong with me stickin' around to keep you company. Just this once."

I smiled and squeezed her shoulder. She didn't punch me, growl like a rabid coyote, nor make any other move or sound that caused me to flinch in mortal terror. If that didn't prove o ur relationship had soared to a new plateau, I didn't know what would.

"Thanks, Thom," I said. "I'm okay, though. Really."

She let out a grunt of reluctant acceptance. "All right, have it your way," she said. And then eyed me a moment. "By the bye, since you brought up

McClintock, what took you so long to get back from his office today?"

I shrugged. I could have sworn *she'd* mentioned his name first. Not that it mattered. Although Mc-Clintock hadn't asked that I keep our talk about Murray confidential, I had a sneaking suspicion he wouldn't appreciate having Thom find out about that conversation. "I don't know," I said. "Guess he wanted to be sure we'd covered all the bases."

"Bases, huh? Like in base*ball*?"

I cleared my throat. Her prying tone immediately made me regret using that particular figure of speech. "I suppose. Don't other sports have bases?"

"None I ever heard of."

"Goes to show you can always learn something new," I said. "Now, if you don't mind, I'd like to start on my work. . . ."

"You go on ahead," she said. "But as a word to the wise, I'd suggest you don't get too personal with the detective."

"Thom, we've had an eventful weekend around here. And he's in charge of investigating the, uh, eventfulness." There, I thought. Now I was flexing my verbal muscles. "What's the problem?"

"I didn't say there was one." She scrutinized me a little more. "I just think it's just best to keep your guard up around him."

"Right, well, I'll remember that if his name and photo pop up during my next eHarmony search . . . if I ever join eHarmony," I said. "In the meantime, I'm scramming upstai—"

"Hang on," she said. "I need to show you something before I forget."

I watched as she went around the front counter, reached underneath it, and brought out Liarson's portfolio.

"What's that doing here?" I said.

"Old Vern found it in the booth where we had our sitdown this morning," she said. "That buzzard lawyer forgot to clean up his droppings. He called while you were gone to tell me he'd return for it, but ain't showed up yet."

"You think he'll be back tonight?"

"I wouldn't be too surprised." Thom looked at me. "The sneaky little runt can't be trusted. He rings the bell, I'd advise you throw the briefcase out the door at him and slam it before he oozes in."

I took the case from her hands, duly warned about detectives and runts. "Might as well bring this upstairs with me," I said.

"Suit yourself." Thom shrugged. "One last item . . . you can use your old key in the side door. It was the jamb that had got splintered and had to be fixed, not the lock."

I nodded, flipped A.J. a little wave so she'd know she could stick her nose back into her own business, and pushed through the kitchen doors toward the stairs.

An hour later, I was sitting at my desk surrounded by lots of open cartons and feeling thwarted. I tried to convince myself that I hadn't been searching for anything in particular, and supposed to some extent it was true. But I'd really been looking for answers as I straightened up the place. Not only that night, but the night before. Somehow or other, I'd hoped to find out what had gotten the restaurant into grave financial trouble.

There had been nothing in the boxes that brought me closer to my goal. I'd found an address book filled with names of wholesalers, which would be handy if I actually stayed in business long enough to order from them. I found loose sheets of paper and Post-its on which Murray had scribbled semi-legible phone numbers, his handwritten supply orders and personal laundry tags, and long to-do lists with all kinds of items that I suspected had never gotten done. I found takeout menus with his partial song lyrics written on their backs, recipes he'd been working on, birthday and holiday cards he'd forgotten to mail, unopened sample bottles from wine, beer, and liquor salesmen. . . .

The discoveries went on and on, but ultimately led to a dead end. By a quarter to nine, I was worn out and vaguely down in the dumps. My bum wrist was sore from shuffling cartons around and my eyes felt grainy with fatigue. I figured it was time to raid the chocolate bowl for some candy and call it quits.

I swiveled around in my chair, looked at the old Gibson guitar case leaning against the wall, and thought about the photo I'd moved downstairs. Murray, me, our victoriously upraised spatulas, my *Schmutz Happens* T-shirt . . . and Murray's thoughtful, loving inscription across the bottom.

*Keep ridin' Gwennie. My heart to yours.*

I swallowed hard over a lump in my throat, my eyes no longer just stinging but moist. I'd been a loser at marriage, and now I was a loser at my new career. My uncle had entrusted me with keeping his dream alive and I'd failed miserably. Feeling guilty about it wouldn't solve anything. Not any more than it would help if I started to cry. It wouldn't help.

I sniffled, pulled a tissue from the box on my desk, and sat there feeling guilty and crying anyway.

"I'm sorry, Murray," I said, staring at the photo through my tears. "Maybe I stink at this deli business. But I've really tried my best to make it work. Tried for you, for me, for both of us."

My teary eyes had remained on the guitar case. Murray had handled it so often, brought it along on so many different gigs, it had always seemed like it was part of him. The red sunburst Gibson he'd kept inside that case was his favorite acoustic, and I could have closed my eyes and seen him strumming one of his original songs on it as if he were right there in front of me, the guitar on his lap, a pick in his left hand.

Moving forward to the edge of my chair, I reached a hand out to touch the case. I couldn't have explained the impulse if someone had asked. Well, okay, that's an outright lie. I could have explained very easily. But it would have made me even more blubbery than I was, and I hated smudging my makeup beyond repair. Fortuitously, however, there was nobody to see me smudge. No one to see my defenses crumble. No one to tell how badly I wanted, *needed,* to feel close to my uncle at that moment.

I was startled when the case tipped over sideways

and fell to the floor. The guitar inside was pretty heavy, not to mention the hardshell case itself, so it should have stood weighted in place. It had been propped there in its spot against the wall since before Murray died. . . .

I didn't understand why it had fallen. But fallen it had. Slid down the wall, hit the floor, bang. Chalk another one up to my klutziness.

Although—

I frowned. It had struck me at once that the bang was *all* I'd heard. Where were the boingy, spoingy notes of protest the guitar should have made on landing?

I bent over to grab the case's handle and stand it upright . . . and realized I hadn't been imagining things. There was no guitar inside. Just a loose, light-weight object I took to be a book of sheet music.

I don't know why this surprised me. In fact, the surprising thing should have been that I hadn't noticed the case was empty sooner. My uncle could have gotten a new case for his guitar. It might have been in his home studio when he died. I hadn't seen it there, but he'd willed most of his instruments to a group of local musicians and it could have been among them. I could ask Artie about it, since he'd been executor of his estate.

Even so, I wondered, why keep an empty guitar case here in the office? And not only that . . .

Murray had been totally self-taught and unable to read a note of written music. I supposed he might have used chord charts when he was young—but that had been long decades ago. He was well, well beyond that as a musician, and could figure out how to play most songs in a blink just by listening to them.

"What on earth would you be doing with sheet music?" I said to the silent room.

Since the room didn't cough up an answer, I decided to try finding one on my own. So, instead of putting the case back where it had leaned against the wall, I carefully set it flat on my desk, unlatched it, raised the lid, and looked inside.

My eyes opened wide. So wide, in fact, that a big, fat, runaway teardrop escaped them and splatted wetly onto the paperwork inside.

My brow creased. The thing I'd heard clunking around inside wasn't a book, but a plain brown 9x12 string-tie envelope. Its front rested flat against the blue felt liner in the wide part of the case, where the guitar's hollow body belonged. There was nothing written on the back of the envelope.

I lifted it out, turned it over. The pair of brief lines in front had been written with a marker pen in Uncle Murray's easily recognizable handwriting, their words all in capitals. The top lines said: CATERING ORDERS/BANK RECEIPTS. Right below it was a single word followed by a question mark: ARTIE?

I stared at the envelope for a long moment, a big, fat, runaway teardrop escaping my eyes to splat wetly onto its surface. Then I unwound its string, opened the flap, and pulled out its contents so I could examine them.

Uncle Murray had been uncharacteristically neat in organizing the paperwork. It appeared he'd taken a full year's catering order forms and sorted them by month, then stapled each month's batch to a bank account statement for that same month. There was nothing fancy or complicated about the forms themselves, which were hard copies of the same electronic ones customers used to book their events online. The first page had the client's name, address, and payment information. The second page was our standard catering menu, basically a pared-down version of our regular restaurant menu. Every selection chosen for the event had a check mark beside it.

Frowning in concentration, I looked over the first bunch of forms. The topmost order had been filled out the previous October by a Ms. Paulina Hardee for a company called Two River Investments. She'd advance-booked a holiday office party for mid-December—forty place settings, a mid-sized bash—and checked off several options for the guests:

### Starters and Side Orders:

- ☑ Steak Fries
  Knishes (round/square)
  - ☑ *Potato*
    *Kasha*
    *Spinach*
    *Mushroom*
  - ☑ *Veggie*
  Kishka
- ☑ Gefilte Fish

## Old-Fashioned Soups:

- ☑ Matzo Ball
  Mama's Chicken
  Chicken Ochre
- ☑ Split Pea

## Classic Hot Sandwiches:

- ☑ Murray's Corned Beef
  Murray's Pastrami
- ☑ Murray's Turkey
  Reuben

## Classic Cold Sandwiches:

- ☑ Murray's Aged In-house Salammi
  Murray's Bologna
  Murray's Tongue
- ☑ Murray's Roast Beef
  Murray's Egg Salad

## Celebrity Entrees:

- ☑ Garth Brooks Prime Cut Brisket
  Merle Haggard Meat Loaf
- ☑ Glen Campbell Crossover Chicken
  and Rib Steak
  George Strait Potato Pancakes with
  Applesauce

Dolly Parton Extra-Loaded Stuffed
Cabbage Rolls

## Desserts:

☑   Homemade Apple Strudel
    Kugel with Hot Fruit Sauce
☑   Fruit Jell-O
☑   Seven Layer Cake
    Rugelach
    Johnny Cashew Pie

My brow furrowed with concentration. At the bottom of the menu, Murray had scratched out several hasty notes and calculations with a pen, and I found myself studying them for a long moment:

*$2,800*   *Tot. (40x$70)*
*$1,400*   *% down. (no bank record online pmnt.)*
*$1,400*   *(See Attched. Bank Stmnt.)*

"There's no record of Ms. Hardee's down payment being deposited into your bank account," I whispered into the silent office. "Why? Where'd it go?"

I flipped the page to the attached monthly bank statement and saw that Murray had circled several deposits, one of which was for the sum of fourteen hundred dollars and dated December eighteenth—a day after the Two Rivers affair. Above it in tiny letters, he'd noted: *Two Rvrs/Hardee. Bal rcvd.*

"So you *did* deposit the balance due, Murray," I mouthed. "Ms. Hardee must've given you a check or credit card payment at the party. But . . ."

But it still left half the money unaccounted for. My hands shaking, I flipped to the next catering order. And the next, and the next, looking for a pattern. It wasn't long before I began to see one emerge—and then become unmistakably clear as the full realization of what I'd discovered overtook me like a tidal wave, a cold sweeping current so powerful, I could barely keep my head above water.

You know that old platitude about the truth setting you free? Well, I felt as if I was drowning in way, *way* too much of it.

"My God," I said, and heard myself pull in a gasping snatch of breath. "My dear God."

Uncle Murray's papers trembling between my fingers, I continued to study them and learn.

# Chapter Nineteen

At a quarter to nine, I was in my office eating a
Three Musketeers bar and waiting. Everyone on the
restaurant's staff had left, and I knew I'd promised
Thomasina I'd be gone by then too.

But I was expecting someone.

As I say, I was waiting.

I wasn't worried about my safety. Maybe it was
stupid and reckless of me. And maybe I would have
been worried if I hadn't been so consumed with
what I'd found out from the papers in Murray's
guitar case. But I had all my rationalizations lined
up in a row. It was barely dark outside. Broadway
was full of pedestrians. And although I'd be at the
restaurant longer than expected, I still didn't intend
to stick around too, too late. If the person I'd called
didn't show up soon, I would go home.

No, I was convinced I wasn't about to do anything rash or stupid.

Maybe—no, probably—I should have known a
whole lot better. But I felt protected.

I glanced down at Uncle Murray's printouts and

bank statements, now spread on the desk in front of me. For about the zillionth time, I found myself appreciating the scrupulous job he'd done. I guessed I wasn't the only member of my family with a knack for accounting. Amazing, though, that it had taken me so long to discover it.

I bit into my chocolate bar and thought about Murray's guitar case hitting the floor without boinging. It was hard for me to explain it away as a coincidence. I still didn't buy the idea of ghosts. I refused to believe there was some invisible Uncle Murray floating around between the kitchen fridge, his office, and possibly even Trudy's C&W club one door down. But I was ready to accept that he'd invested so much of himself in the restaurant that some essence of his spirit remained after his death. I could feel it around me; I honestly could. It gave me a kind of confidence. Made me all the more determined to set the record straight about him.

I'd been supposed to think Murray's airheadedness and supposed disorganization were the reasons for its declining profitability. It had seemed to me I could have taken my pick of explanations, fished any one I wanted from the pickle barrel, as long as it pointed to the deli's losses being Murray's fault.

It was five to nine when the bell rang downstairs. We didn't have one in front, but there was a buzzer at the side door. I guessed the man I was expecting could have let himself in—he was one of the people who had a key. And maybe someone who could have been responsible for locking me inside the refrigerator. But I couldn't bring myself to blame him for deliberately trying to hurt me or anybody else. For other things, yes. Just not those things.

I pushed the rest of the chocolate bar into my mouth, picked my cell phone up off the desk, thumbed to its voice recorder function without activating it, and put it back down. Then I took my compact from my bag and looked in the mirror to make sure my reapplied makeup was perfect and my eyes weren't still bloodshot from crying. I'd used Visine to get the redness out of them.

As a finishing touch, I pursed my lips to ensure my lipstick was nice and even. Everything about me looked hunky-dory. I was one low-down, ready-for-a-showdown five-foot-four Northern shrimp.

I hurried downstairs to answer the buzzer, pausing in the dimness of the kitchen as I remembered my run-in with the walk-in. I could feel a rapid heartbeat in my chest, but wasn't really frightened or anxious. It was mostly anticipation—I wanted things over and done.

Swinging around to the left of the stairs, I went to the side loading door, pulled it open . . . and blinked in surprise.

The man standing out in the alley wasn't the one I'd expected. "Liarson," I said. "What are you doing here?"

"I've come for my briefcase," he said. "Weren't you told I accidentally left it behind this morning?"

I sighed. Right, I thought. The truth was that I'd been so preoccupied, it had momentarily slipped my mind.

I knew that Cazzie and Thom would have warned me against letting him through the door. But if he'd already sneaked in once on Saturday night, he could have easily done it again tonight—and he hadn't. And suppose he *had* planned on doing me harm . . . why would he call to announce he was returning for his portfolio? All that would do if anything happened to me was make Liarson a prime suspect.

No, I didn't think I had anything to fear from him. Detestable as he was.

"The case is in my office," I said with a nod over my shoulder. "Follow me."

We went upstairs, Liarson close behind me. I'd dropped the briefcase on a carton by my desk, and he waited a step or two inside the door as I got it for him.

"You know, Ms. Silver, our differences should not have to take a personal slant."

"Thanks for informing me," I said.

"I'm quite serious," Liarson said. "Sooner or later, Ramsey Holdings will gain control of this property. That much is inevitable. And then . . . perhaps things will change between us."

I turned, handed Liarson the briefcase. "Change how?" I said. "Not that it's *going* to happen."

"Change for the better," he said, and smiled like a rat eyeing a wedge of cheese. "Change in ways we both might find enjoyable."

I looked at him, thinking I might be nauseous. Maybe it *had* been a mistake letting him through the door. "Wasn't it just this morning that my cashier told you to put your married eyes back in your married head? Because you were checking *her* out?"

"That was nothing but errant libido," he said. "My attraction to you is profoundly different. We are alphas, you and I. A lion and lioness. You excite me like no other woman I've ever met."

"I'm sure your wife would be thrilled."

Liarson smiled, tilted his head sideways. I thought maybe it was supposed to be a rakish angle. "What my wife doesn't know can't hurt her," he said.

*Ugh.* I wondered how often my ex had used that line on his pole dancers. "Listen, I think you ought to leave this second. In fact, I wish you could retroactively leave so I wouldn't have to remember you hitting on me."

"I will do as you wish," he said. Although I didn't notice him budge from where he stood with his back to my open door. "But please be aware of something, Ms. Silver. I'm an attorney by profession, but a man of many passions. Art, cinema, curling . . . there is much in which we can delight together."

I looked at him. *Curling?* Things had gone from peculiar to downright bizarre.

"Okay, you twerp, that's about all I can stand," I said, pointing at the door behind him. "I'm telling you right now, you've got about three seconds to— *lookout!*"

But my warning was too late. it had barely escaped my lips when I saw an upraised gun appear in the doorway behind Liarson, then come swinging down hard to crack him hard in the back of his head. As his body crumpled to the floor in a pile, his eyes rolling up in their sockets, I took a giant step back from the doorway . . . and the man who'd suddenly appeared on the other side of it.

"Artie," I said, seeing him framed in the entry for the first time. "What are you doing?"

He stepped over Liarson and into the office, the pistol held out in front of him. Black and smooth, I thought it was a Glock of the sort policemen carried around. "There's no reason to be surprised," he said. "You asked me to come here after all."

I kept backing away, moving toward my desk, my hands out behind me.

"Stop right there," he said. Pushing the gun in the air. "Don't take another step."

I didn't have to. In fact, I couldn't. I'd come right up against my desk so I could feel its edge pressing against my spine. I stood there between Artie and the phone I'd left on the desktop, blocking it from his sight, and moved my hands behind my back, groping with my outstretched fingers.

"What are you doing?" he said.

"Nothing," I said. "I—"

"I want to see your hands," he said. "Don't screw around with me, Gwen. I'm no clown like that lawyer."

I pushed what I hoped was the record button on my keypad, dropped my arms straight down at my sides.

"Artie," I said. "It shouldn't have to come to this. Not after all these years."

"What else is left, Gwen?" he said. "You found the bank statements. The printouts of the catering orders. Isn't that what you told me?"

I had. And when I'd compared the total amounts due for the events to the money actually deposited in the restaurant's bank account—no, strike that, when my *uncle* had compared them—none of the deposits were more than half of what should have been taken in. In fact, it became clear they only covered the balances Murray received on the day of the events. In the two years since Artie's online system had gone operational, the down payments for each and every catered function at the deli had simply disappeared. It had added up to over seventy thousand dollars in gross receipts.

Seventy thousand dollars, diverted . . . *where?*

The answer had become pretty obvious to me. As it must have to my uncle.

"It's so insidious, Artie," I said. "You talk Murray into a computerized system for his catering events. Set it up for him. And then what? Funnel the down payments into your personal account? That's fifty percent of the gross carved right off the top. Fifty percent at a very *minimum* . . ."

"That's enough," he said. "You must have been a great forensic accountant in New York. Because you've got it down pat. I took the damned money, and so what?"

I looked at him. Not just hoping I'd hit the right button on my phone, but praying now. "Why, Artie?" I said. "Why'd you do it? Help me understand."

Artie's lips tightened as he came closer with the outthrust gun. "I'm a human being. I have expenses. And beyond that, I have desires," he said. "Look at it from my vantage, Gwen. I see your uncle passing out cash to every stumblebum guitar-picker who hits him up for a loan. Every one of them. And he doesn't even care if he gets it back." He chuckled. "Why even bother calling them loans? Handouts, that's what they were. Meanwhile, I've got to live on a salary. Work day and night to make sense of the notes Murray left here, there, and everywhere. Sit in front of spreadsheets." He shook his head. "I used to be a *drummer,* Gwen."

"And Murray was a guitarist. A songwriter . . ."

"But he always had his cooking. If music was his wife, the cooking was his mistress. And he loved both of them," Artie said. "This restaurant was *his* dream, not mine."

"So I'm guessing you weren't too disappointed when Royce Ramsey made his buyout offer."

Artie's mouth turned down in a sneer. "You have your nerve, judging me."

"I wasn't—"

"Don't lie, Gwen. I can see what you think of me in your *eyes,*" Artie said. "Yeah, sure, Ramsey's offer was the clincher. I've got my little share of the deli. Thomasina too. It could have put us on easy street for the rest of our lives. And Murray turned him down."

"Thom didn't seem to mind."

"What do you expect?" Artie snapped. "Your uncle was *sleeping* with her."

I felt sorrow cut into my heart like a knife. "Murray practically considered you his brother. The two of you go back so far . . . I bet it tore him apart to find out you were stealing from him."

"Tore him apart?" Artie made an odd snuffling noise and stepped closer with the gun. It took me a moment to see the tears on his face. "The stupid fool, it gave him a heart attack. *Killed* him. He got so mad . . . told me I should have just asked for the money. That I should've come begging to him like those moochers. As if he shouldn't have taken

care of me first. As if I wasn't his partner of thirty
years. His best friend. His brother, like you said."

I should have been terrified. I know I should
have. But all I felt was that deep, piercing sadness
in my heart. "Artie," I said. "Artie . . . you should
have just talked to him."

Tears flowing freely down his cheeks, he came
closer and closer with the gun till it was just inches
away, aimed directly at me, his finger curled
around its trigger. "Big New Yorker, you got all the
answers. If you'd just eaten your brisket instead of
Sergeant, it would've solved everything."

My eyes grew enormous. "You poisoned the
beef?"

"That's right. That brisket's your usual dinner,
Gwen. Everybody knows it. But your portion must've
gotten mixed up with Sergeant's," Artie sobbed. I
could hear his hitching breaths and see the tears
continue to spill from his eyes, splashing over his
lips and chin. "I got that stuff they use on predators
from some cattleman out in the sticks. Furadan. I
was at his ranch doing his taxes for extra cash, saw
him use it when the wildlife rangers turned their
backs, and took some home with me."

I stared at him as if the pistol wasn't between us.
The whole scattered puzzle—its pieces were suddenly coming together in my mind. "You used your
key to get in the restaurant's side door. Acted as if
you were rushing upstairs for some paperwork,
then injected some poison into the beef right under
everybody's noses. No one there paid attention or
even noticed you passing through the kitchen. Because you do it all the time."

"Right, Gwen. All the time." Artie was nodding his head. "Thing is, I wouldn't be doing this right now if you'd decided to sell your share of the restaurant and stay in New York. I'm the executor of Murray's will. You die, I'll take care of Thomasina next. And then I'll control what happens to this place. And I can unload it on Ramsey the way your uncle should have."

I stood with my back against the desk. I'd gotten my statement recorded. Hurray for me. But there was nowhere left to go now. Nowhere.

"What good will it do you to kill me now?" I said. "I can't see how shooting me gains you anything—"

"I'm not going to shoot you." He nodded his head back at Liarson's prostrate form. "He will."

I shook my head uncomprehendingly.

"Don't look so confused," Artie said. "It's all neat and tidy. Couldn't have worked out better. He comes up here to take you out of the picture, the two of you fight over his gun, and you're shot point-blank in the chest. But you manage to wrestle it away from Liarson, stay alive long enough to put a bullet in him . . . and both of you wind up dead."

I looked at him, my mouth dry. Artie was sweating profusely, despair and anger playing over his face, pulling it into a grimacing, distorted mask as he lowered the Glock so it was level with my heart.

And then I saw a shadow fill the doorway behind him. A huge, square, *beehived* shadow.

*She didn't listen to me!* I thought, my heart jumping in my rib cage. *Of course, she didn't! She never listens!*

I looked past Artie, and for the second time since coming upstairs shouted a warning because of someone at the door. "Careful! He's got a gun!"

Artie snorted. "You think I'll fall for that old chestnut? Little girl, you've seen *way* too many cowboy movies—"

"Well, I don't *think* so!" Thomasina shouted out, storming through the door just as he turned toward the sound of her voice, planting herself squarely on both feet to hit him solidly across the jaw with a wide, looping roundhouse haymaker.

Artie's eyes had no sooner showed his astonishment than they rolled up in his head from the blow. He groaned in pain and slumped on his buckled knees, struggling to remain upright . . . and then Thomasina stepped into him and reared back again, her second punch walloping his nose with an audible crunch.

The pistol dropping from his grip, he spun around in a half circle, staggering drunkenly, tripping backward over one of the open cartons, to finally land on top of Liarson, his arms and legs flopping in different directions.

"That one was for Murray, you schemin' toad," Thom said, rubbing her knuckles as she looked down at him. Then she raised her eyes to my face. "You okay, Princess?"

I nodded that I was and gave her a thin smile. "I thought I told you to go on home."

"Good thing I never pay attention to you, huh?"

"Yeah," I said. "Good thing."

Thom looked at me. "Truth be told, I was half-way there on the interstate when I decided to turn back," she said. "Next time Thomasina wants to stick around, you listen to what she says. 'Cause these trips back and forth to check up on you waste *way* too much money and gas!"

For once, I had no witty comebacks. Underneath Artie's tangled arms and legs, Liarson briefly lifted his head off the floor and gave me a foggy, semi-conscious look. *"Currrrrling, sexy,"* he slurred, then conked out again.

Thom looked at me. "What was that came out of his mouth?"

I sighed, wiped the tears from my eyes with my bandaged wrist. "Trust me, it isn't worth repeating," I said.

# Chapter Twenty

When Detective McClintock strode into the deli Monday morning, I was in the middle of booking a reservation for a party of four. The phone behind the register was ringing off the hook, the row of buttons under the touch pad flashing nonstop. It had been the same since I'd arrived for work.

I held up a finger to McClintock, noted the booking down on our calendar, and passed the receiver to Luke so he could take the next caller. Then I slid along the counter to where McClintock was waiting for me.

"Whoa," I said. "Deep-breath time. I thought I'd never get away from that phone."

McClintock grinned. "Why the big rush on deli food?"

"Today's paper," I said. And got a blank look in return. "You mean you didn't see the newspaper?"

He shook his head no. "We've had a frenzy going at headquarters too."

I reached under the counter for my early edition of the *Nashville Times*.

"Here," I said, and held it up on display. "Take a look."

McClintock made a whistling noise as he scanned the front page. There were split photos of Artie Duff, Royce Ramsey and Cyrus Liarson near the top. Below them, surrounded by article copy, was a shot of the deli taken from directly out front on Broadway—with an insert picture of me in the window. The banner headline read:

## A RARE BREED OF KATZ

### Heroine Deli Owner Gwen Katz
### Solves Sergeant Murder,
### Saved by Hostess in Sunday Dustup

"Loud but accurate," McClintock said. "Seems they got your last name wrong, though."

I shrugged, put the paper down. "I was planning to drop the 'Silver' anyway," I said. "It's about time I shook it once and for all."

McClintock looked at me, smiled. "Gwen Katz," he said. "I kind of like it."

"Guess the rest of Nashville does too," I said, and gestured at the crowd of people waiting for tables. "Though I think it's really the 'heroine' tag that's got business jumping. A couple of days ago, the restaurant was a house of horror. Now it's a local attraction. Everybody wants to meet the crime-solving owner and her rock-'em-sock-'em hostess partner."

McClintock laughed. "And how's Thomasina been affected by her fifteen minutes of fame?"

"I ain't changed no way, Beau McClintock . . . and that especially goes for my view of men like you. Which'll stick with me long after that fifteen minutes has gone into the dumper."

He looked over his shoulder toward where she stood by her podium. "It's always a pleasure to see you, Thom."

"I won't be a fake and tell you likewise."

McClintock frowned. "I guess celebrity really hasn't softened you."

"You think I was lyin' when I told you so?" She crossed her arms, staring at him. "I'll soften when you give me a reason, Beau. But right now I'd appreciate you keepin' your business here short. The place is packed to the rafters and we can't have you blockin' the ais—"

Thom broke off as a new group of customers arrived at the door to further clog the entrance. She reached over to grab the waiting list from her podium and went over to greet them . . . but not before giving McClintock a parting look of antagonism.

"So," I said, feeling a little sorry for him. "What brings you here?"

He stuck a hand into his jacket pocket and produced my cell phone. "I wanted to return this to you for one thing," he said. "There's no need for us to hang onto it now that we've copied your audio file and logged it as evidence."

"And the recording's okay?" I asked. "I mean, you think it'll hold up in court?"

"Gwen, you got Artie Duff basically laying out how he embezzled from the restaurant, poisoned

Buster Sergeant, and planned to shoot you and Liarson in cold blood," McClintock said. "The only thing better would be a formal confession . . . and from the way he's been crying in his cell all night, I suspect he'll give us one eventually. I've been at my job long enough to recognize a man who's torn up inside with guilt."

I looked at McClintock a moment. "Thank you, Beau," I said. "You've been a huge help through a rough ordeal."

He seemed genuinely surprised. "It was you that made the recording, Gwen. And Thom who kayoed Artie in the nick of time. I hardly feel like I did much of anything."

"How about showing me kindness and consideration? And pulling me out of the refrigerator the other night? And following me home to make sure I got there safe?" I said. "If it wasn't for you mentioning how important it is to get people's direct statements, I'd never have thought of it."

McClintock just shrugged that off. "I just wish I'd been keeping watch over the deli last night when Artie showed. Maybe then I'd deserve credit. But as it stands—"

I held up a hand. Luke had come over with the phone and tapped me on the shoulder. "It's for you, Nash," he said, his voice raised over the hubbub of waiting diners.

"Can you take a message?" I asked.

Luke cupped a hand over the mouthpiece. "It's Royce Ramsey," he said. "Claims it's urgent business."

I frowned, looked at McClintock. "I probably

should answer this one. It's my good friend, Mr. Ra—"

"I heard," he said. And lowered his voice confidentially. "If you don't mind my waiting around, I'd like to ask you a personal question once you're finished with him."

I nodded, took the phone. "Hello?"

"Ms. Silver?"

"It's Katz now," I said. "In case you didn't see this morning's paper."

"I did indeed," Ramsey said. "Katz . . . that's your maiden name, yes? I didn't know you'd gone back to using it."

"Well, it's understandable, since I didn't tell you," I said. And then couldn't resist sticking it to him. "I just figured that with all the reservations we're getting today—and there are more than we can handle—our diners should know without a doubt that I'm Murray Katz's niece. And that this deli's going to be owned and operated by a Nashville Katz for a long time to come."

I wasn't sure what sort of reaction I expected from Ramsey. But since needling him had been my single, solitary goal, his laughter came as an annoying surprise.

"I say something funny?"

"It seems you do all the time," Ramsey answered. "Ms. Katz, I confess you are a pure delight. A breath of fresh air in Nashville."

"Glad you think so. Because I plan on sticking around here." I admit that I was still trying to get a rise out of him. "Business is good at the deli. Our star's bright again, Mr. Ramsey. And whatever plans you might have for your ingeniously named

Ramsey Land, you can forget about getting your hands on this restaurant."

Ramsey paused at the other end of the line. "Well, Ms. Katz, I hate to argue with you, so I suggest we leave that to the future," he said. "In the meantime . . . what would you say to dinner?"

My eyebrows scrunched. With all the commotion around me, I thought maybe I'd heard him wrong. I covered my ear to block out some of the noise.

"Excuse me . . . did you say *dinner*?"

"That's right."

"Mr. Ramsey . . . you must be joking."

"Why?" he said. "We might be on opposite sides of a particular issue. But I believe I've always been a gentleman with you."

"Well . . ."

"That is, I've certainly tried to be one despite our differences."

I sighed. "I can't say you haven't been," I said reluctantly.

"Then why not see how we do over what we have in common?"

"Mr. Ramsey," I said, "I'm glad we're being civil. But—"

"I'm sorry, can you speak up? There must be some kind of ruckus at your end, because I can't hear you too well."

"I said that I'm pleased we can have a civil relationship," I said, raising my voice. "As far as the two of us going out on a *date,* though—"

I noticed McClintock looking across the counter at me, realized he must have heard that, and rolled my eyes to telegraph my incredulity. "Look, Mr. Ramsey—"

"Royce."

"Royce," I said. "I must tell you, it makes me uncomfortable that you've asked me. . . ."

"To have dinner under the stars at my hacienda," Ramsey said. "This Friday night."

"Yeah, I heard you, starlight and romance," I said. "Assuming you're serious, the fact is, it's totally inappropriate—"

"With a mariachi band playing, and a bottle of fine wine between us," he said.

I took a deep breath, shaking my head. Ramsey definitely had his nerve. In fact, nerve wasn't even the word for it. For God's sake, he'd tried to steal my restaurant. His nice, genuine laugh and gentlemanliness notwithstanding, the man was a crumb.

"This is ridiculous," I said, a little embarrassed to see that McClintock was still watching me. "My answer's n—"

"What is there to lose by taking a chance, Gwen?" Ramsey said. "The only things I've ever regretted in life are missed opportunities . . . and I've learned not to let them go by."

I hesitated, my tongue stuck to the roof of my mouth. A crumb, I thought. A feather-crested crumb. And yet . . .

No, I told myself. I would not be tempted. I'd give him his answer and *how.*

"Okay, Royce, Friday night, we're on," I said to my own stunned disbelief. And then hung up the phone, looked across the counter, and realized McClintock had started toward the door.

"Beau, I thought you wanted to ask me something?" I called after him.

He paused, looked at me with the crowd milling around him. "It'll wait," he said. "No big deal. See you around, Gwen."

A moment later, McClintock went walking out the door, which not only left me confused about why he'd left in such a hurry, but also made me wonder.

It wasn't as if I was some kind of soap opera vamp all of a sudden. I really, emphatically do not like drama. But by a personal question . . . was it *possible* that he'd meant . . . ?

Staring out the window, I watched McClintock turn toward police headquarters and then vanish down the street. And before I could wonder about him too much longer, the phone rang and I picked it up. It was a wholesale meat distributor—I'd left a message for him after seeing his outfit listed in Murray's contact book. The guy had a quality pastrami to sell me. And he swore he meant a pastrami that wasn't a pig.

I ordered it from him and took the next call. And the next, and then the next. The day was rolling along in high gear, customers flowing in the door, deli smells wafting from the kitchen—cured meat and knishes, roasts and toasting bagels.

Yup, as I'd told Ramsey, business was good. Murray's Deli was there for the duration. And so was I.

# RECIPES
# FROM MURRAY'S
# DELICATESSEN

## Recipe 1
## Murray's Cholent (Crock-Pot)

This is the quintessential Eastern European Jewish meal with some added Southern smokiness and kick. It may be served with A.J.'s Corn Bread.

### Ingredients

2 pounds rib eye roast cut into pieces
1 cup high-quality spicy salami (diced)
1½ cups dry mixed beans
(red kidney, black, white navy, etc.)
1¼ cups pearled barley
3–4 potatoes, peeled and cut in large chunks
1 large onion, coarsely chopped
2 stalks celery, coarsely chopped
1 pound baby carrots
5 cloves garlic, minced
¼ cup chopped parsley

2 cups dry red wine
2 tablespoons honey
2 tablespoons vegetable oil
Water (enough to cover 1 inch above ingredients)

## Seasoning Mix

1 tablespoon kosher salt
1½ tablespoons Hungarian paprika
1 teaspoon onion powder
1 teaspoon garlic powder
1 teaspoon cumin
1 teaspoon black pepper
1 teaspoon ancho chile pepper
½ teaspoon white pepper
½ teaspoon cayenne pepper
3 bay leaves

## Instructions

Wash the beans thoroughly and soak them for at least 8 hours. Drain. In an iron pan, heat the oil, brown all sides of the rib eye, and set it aside. Mix the seasonings and set them aside. Arrange the onions, celery, garlic, and parsley over the bottom of the Crock-Pot. Add the bay leaves. Add the rib eye and salami and pour ½ of the seasoning mix over the meat, spreading it as evenly as possible. Add the potatoes and carrots and evenly spread the *remaining* seasoning mix over them. Place the pearl barley and beans on top of the meat. Add the wine and honey. Bring water to a boil and add it to the Crock-Pot. Turn the Crock-Pot to high and cook overnight. Shortly before serving the cholent, turn the Crock-Pot to low, check the water level, and add a little more water if it seems low. Invite the neighborhood and chow down!

Tip: Unpeeled potatoes hang onto their shape, flavor, and vitamins better than peeled potatoes, so if you don't mind the peels, leave them on. Also, red potatoes can be substituted for regular potatoes to add color to the dish.

# Recipe 2
# Newt's Chicken Okra Soup

Newt's family was originally from Louisiana, and he suggested giving a Cajun flair to this variation on a traditional Jewish chicken soup recipe. Murray's only stipulation: NO PORK!

## Ingredients

1½ pounds chicken thighs
1½ cups fresh okra (cut into ½-inch slices)
2 stalks celery, sliced
1 medium onion, chopped
1 green bell pepper, chopped
4 cloves garlic, minced
1 eight-ounce can tomato sauce
⅓ cup uncooked rice
1 teaspoon olive oil

## Seasonings

1½ teaspoons salt
1 teaspoon paprika
1 teaspoon ground cumin
½ teaspoon dried basil
½ teaspoon black pepper
¼ teaspoon white pepper
¼ teaspoon red pepper (cayenne preferred)
2 bay leaves

## Instructions

Cover the bottom of a pan with the olive oil and place over a high heat. When the oil is very hot, add the onions and celery and sauté approximately 3 minutes or until the vegetables are golden brown. Add the minced garlic, sauté 30 seconds, and remove from heat.

Place the chicken thighs, broth, tomato sauce, salt, paprika, cumin, garlic, black pepper, white pepper, and red pepper in a large pot. Bring the soup to a full boil over high heat, then decrease the heat to medium and let it simmer, uncovered, for 1 hour or until the chicken is tender. Skim whatever foam rises to the surface. When the chicken is tender, remove it from the soup and set it aside until it is cool enough to handle. Remove the chicken meat from the skin and bones, cut the meat into bite-sized pieces, and discard the skin and bones. Add the chicken, chopped green bell pepper, and rice to the soup and bring to a boil. Reduce heat to low-medium and simmer uncovered 10 minutes or until rice is tender. Add okra, simmer an additional 8 minutes or until okra is tender. Ladle soup into bowls and dig in!

Tips: If you'd like more heat, add a dash of Tabasco sauce. A garnish of fresh parsley or green onion slivers adds a little spring color to the soup.

## Recipe 3
## Full of Bologna Sandwich

Try this for a quick, easy, and delicious lunch. It's a hearty sandwich at a manageable bite-sized height, and everything stays neatly in place since the sliced bologna and roll are the same shape. As Murray always said, "Anybody who likes a hot dog *has* to love this sandwich!"

### Ingredients

1 small onion
4–5 slices bologna (medium thickness)
1 hard roll (sliced for sandwich)
Mustard (optional)

### Instructions

Slice the onion to a medium thickness. Heat the oil in a large iron frying pan or grill, using just enough to cover the bottom of the pan so the onions and bologna won't stick. When the pan is heated, toss in the sliced onions and cook them till they're translucent but *not* brown. Add the bologna slices and cook them until they pop up like helmets. (Picture those American M1 World War Two army helmets—seriously!) Turn the bologna slices over with a fork or tongs—being careful not to tear them—and cook their other sides until they pop up. Now smear the mustard on the underside of the top half of the roll, stack the bologna on the bottom of the sliced roll, and pile on the onions. Finally, dig in while it's still hot!

Tip: To round off and add garden freshness to your meal, serve the Full of Bologna Sandwich with sliced cherry tomatoes sprinkled with chopped parsley and coarse salt.

## Recipe 4
## A.J.'s Tennessee Corn Bread

Southerners serve corn bread as a side order with just about every dish, and it's as delicious with deli food as any other. A.J. uses a mix of brown sugar and white sugar for added home-style sweetness. Her variation also uses finely chopped jalapenos to give it some nice heat, but they can be left out for a more traditional corn bread flavor.

### Ingredients

1 cup yellow cornmeal
1 cup all-purpose flour
½ cup good aged cheddar cheese (hand-grated)
5 jalapenos (finely chopped)
$1/3$ cup white sugar
$1/3$ cup brown sugar
1 teaspoon salt
3½ teaspoons baking powder
1 egg
1 cup whole milk
$1/3$ cup vegetable oil

### Instructions

Preheat the oven to 400 degrees F. Lightly grease a 9-inch round cake pan. In a large bowl, mix the cornmeal, flour, sugar, salt, and baking powder. Stir in the egg, milk, and vegetable oil until they're well combined. Then add the cheddar and jalapenos and stir so they're evenly distributed throughout the batter. Pour the batter into the pan and bake in the oven for 20 to 25 minutes or until a toothpick inserted into the center of the loaf pulls out clean. The corn bread should be cut into 2-inch squares and served warm with anything and everything. And if you're feeling extra indulgent, you can smear on some butter and honey.

## Recipe 5
## Old-Fashioned Noodle Kugel

Kugel is a German-Jewish noodle pudding whose origins go back almost a millennium. While many varieties have evolved over the years, here's the basic recipe Grandma used. At Murray's Deli, we offer it to those who crave a traditional comfort food as a side dish or dessert. It's perfect with roasts, meat loaf, soups, and sandwiches . . . but don't miss the chance to have a piece on its lonesome with a nice, steaming cup of coffee!

## Ingredients

1 package (8 oz.) wide noodles
½ pound cottage cheese
4 tablespoons cream cheese
½ cup sour cream or whole milk yogurt
1 heaping tablespoon sugar
4 egg whites, or 2 whole eggs beaten
½ stick unsalted butter (melted)
½ teaspoon natural vanilla
(no artificial stuff, please!)

## Topping

½ cup plain bread crumbs
1½ teaspoon brown sugar
½ teaspoon cinnamon
1 tablespoon unsalted butter (melted)

## Instructions

Cook noodles according to the directions on the package. (Be careful not to overcook because you'll be popping the kugel into the oven.) When noodles are cooked, place them in a large mixing bowl and set aside.

In a medium-size mixing bowl, combine and mix the next four ingredients: cottage cheese, cream cheese, sour cream (or whole yogurt), and sugar. Set this mix aside.

In another medium-size bowl, mix the eggs (or egg whites), butter, and vanilla.

Now combine all the ingredients in the large mixing bowl that holds the noodles. Fold the ingredients together thoroughly. Place them in a large (8-inch) square brownie pan that has been spritzed with cooking spray. Preheat the oven to 350 degrees F and take a breather. Don't worry, though, you're almost there.

Mix all topping ingredients together (plain bread crumbs, brown sugar, cinnamon, and unsalted butter) in another bowl. Evenly sprinkle this mixture on top of the kugel, put it in the preheated oven, and bake uncovered for about an hour. Remove when you think the top looks crunchy (but not dry).

Tip: For bursts of fruity sweetness, you can add ¼ cup raisins to the kugel—simply stir them into the egg, butter, and vanilla mix; the rest of your preparation stays the same. At Murray's, we prefer flame raisins because they're large, plump, and generally stay moist, but any type of raisin will do.

# KITCHEN TIPS
# FROM THE PROS

Here are a few useful pointers from the kitchen crew at Murray's Deli.

1) Zipper storage bags are great for marinating. Just place marinade and meat in a bag, close it tightly, set it in a shallow dish, and put it in the refrigerator—that's it! No tools, no mess. When the meat needs turning, flip the bag over and give it a few squeezes to distribute the marinade.

2) It's a good idea to keep a box of instant potatoes on hand in case your soup, stew, or gravy needs some thickening. Add a small amount of the instant potatoes at a time, stir, let it cook, and continue adding in increments until the liquid reaches the consistency you desire.

3) You can keep your celery crisp in one of two ways. Either cut the stalks and place them in a glass of cold, salted water, or wrap them tightly in aluminum foil and store them in the fridge.

4) Speaking of the fridge—be careful of what you freeze! Leftovers containing garlic or peppers will taste a bit stronger once they've been frozen.

5) If you bake in glass pans, the light-colored pans are the best. Darker colors bake hotter.

6) Keep your pizza wheel handy even when there's no pie around. It's great for slicing grilled cheese and many other toasted delights.

7) When making your favorite coleslaw, add some slices of green pepper for a fresh garden taste.

8) One frequently asked question is, "What's the difference between frying in a little oil and sautéing?" The answer is, "For the most part, 'sauté' *sounds* better!"

9) Nonprofessional cooks tend to slice their meat with the grain, but you might have

noticed that most restaurants serve meat that's been sliced *against* the grain. We recommend that as a standard practice. Even a thin portion of meat will hold together better when it is sliced against the grain. You'll have a nice presentation and it's easier to eat.

10) A major don't-forget-type tip is that, pound for pound, a boneless roast takes longer to cook than a roast with a bone. The bone acts as a heat core carrying the heat to the center of the roast.

Turn the page for a preview of


ONE FOOT IN THE GRAVY
A Nashville Katz Mystery
By Delia Rosen

Coming in October 2011
Where books are sold

# Chapter One

"The Creeping Leeches?" said Thomasina. "Oh my Lawfy, what kinda sick, disgustin' name is that?"

I eyed the logo on the side of the van. Although Thom's reading of it wasn't *quite* errorless, her reaction was definitely understandable. I had worries of my own about the realistic painted leeches forming the letters being enough to kill people's appetites. But transportation was transportation; we couldn't afford to be choosy.

Thom should have known making a fuss wouldn't help. Then again, when had knowing better than to complain ever stopped her? Under *any* circumstance?

Luke frowned at her from the driver's seat. Moments earlier, he'd swung into the alley between my restaurant and the country-and-western night club next door, pulling to a halt in front of the service and delivery entrance. With an unlit cigarette poking from my mouth—I was trying to gratify my oral fixation while quitting the habit cold turkey—I'd been waiting there with my grumpy manager for about fifteen minutes.

"Before you criticize, Thom, you oughtta try 'n read it right," he said through his lowered passenger window. "Ain't no 'the' in it. And it's written *CreepLeeches*—one word—for a reason."

"And what might that reason be?"

"Reason's that the rockabilly group that owns the van ought to know how they want their name spelled. And you're lookin' at their official tour vehicle."

"That so?"

"You better believe it," Luke said. "And stickin' to the point, you got to have some respect. A name's a name. Like mine's Luke. Like yours is Thomasina Jackson. And like Nash here's, well, y'know . . ."

Luke scratched under his ear, realizing I wasn't the best example he could have chosen. With me stuff always gets a little complicated. F'rinstance, Nash was short for Nashville Katz, my full nickname. The "Nashville" part referred to the location of my restaurant—Murray's—which happened to be the first and only Jewish deli in Music City. The "Katz" part came from my *real* name, Gwen Katz. And the whole thing was a play on the title of some old Lovin' Spoonful song that unquestionably could have been written about my late uncle Murray, from whom I'd inherited the place right before my messy, humiliating New York divorce from the Pied Piper of Stripper-land was finalized.

Told you it was tricky, didn't I?

"Okay, we better forget Nash," Luke said. He

was still looking out at Thom. "I want to hear where you figure we'd be if CreepLeeches hadn't loaned us their van."

"Inside, where we belong, preparin' for dinner . . . and if you don't stop repeatin' that awful name I'm gonna puke!" Thom replied. "Say what you want, I ain't a deliverywoman for some rich old crackpot."

I checked my watch and decided it was time to interrupt. As much as they enjoyed bickering with each other, we had to get cracking. "Easy, Thom, that's unfair," I said. "Lolo Baker's a nice lady."

"One who's got nothin' better to do with her nights than playact with her friends."

"Don't change the subject. We were talking about her dinner party—"

"*Murder* party," Thom interrupted. "You ought to be clear about what it is while tryin' to persuade me that she ain't batty."

"And you ought to stop being so obnoxious," I said.

Thom's brow furrowed under her bob of silver hair. "What's that supposed to mean?"

I sighed. "It means it's ridiculous for us to argue about this. Audience participation dinner shows are mega-popular everywhere. And Lolo's into reading murder mysteries. I think her throwing a mystery-themed dinner is a fun idea."

"Well, I think it's trouble," she said. "She can get half-naked men in Spartacus costumes to serve her food for all I care. But since when are *we* in the caterin' business?"

"Since Lolo offered to pay us big time."

"Then you admit this is about her havin' oodles of money."

"Did I ever tell you it hurt? You know how much we're taking in for the party. Businesses have to grow—"

"Says who?" Thom frowned disapprovingly. "In all the years he owned the deli, Murray never mentioned a word about growin'."

"Maybe that's true," I said. "But things change."

"And how might that be? How's *any*thing different besides you bein' in charge nowadays? And your boyfriend, Royce Ramsey, wantin' to buy us out."

I looked at her. "That isn't fair. It's been six months since Royce approached us. And furthermore, he isn't my boyfriend."

"Oh no?" Her tone went from critical to knowing. "Then what you gonna call him, sugar?"

The phrase *unstoppable turbocharged sex dynamo* jumped into my head, but I wasn't sure that would help make my case. "If you want to mudwrestle, count me out," I replied instead. "I shouldn't have to remind you that our insurance premiums went sky high after the flood. With rates being what they are, we can use some added revenue. And special events planning is just an extension of what we already do. It isn't as if this is totally unfamiliar territory."

Thom stood there scowling at me a few seconds. Then she nodded back toward the van. "Might I ask how rollin' up to Brentwood in that eyesore's gonna make us look? Or you really think Lolo's a fan 'a the Slime Bugs?"

"CreepLeeches!" Luke shouted out his window.

"I'd suggest you get that straight, because the band's got itself a huge followin'."

"Yeah? In what *swamp?*"

"You ain't the slightest bit funny." Luke shook his head. "People do us a favor, we ought to be grateful. My cousin Zach and his boys were even kind enough to remove their instruments—well, except for a drum kit and some cables, I guess—so we'd have plenty of room for food."

"Speaking of which," I said, tapping my watch, "we'd better get ready to roll."

Thom looked at me. "So you really intend to go through with this harebrained deal?"

"Right you are, Thom. We're professionals, and whatever you might think this job's important to us. I have absolutely no intention of blowing it."

She opened her mouth to answer, then seemed to change her mind. It was almost two o'clock on a Saturday afternoon and the murder mystery dinner was set for seven P.M. Moreover, we'd booked it several weeks before. Her grumbling aside, Thomasina really was as professional as they came. She would have never backed out—or expected *me* to back out—at that late stage.

Losing the sour puss was another story, of course, and I was getting a serious eyeful it when the service door swung open and Newt—that's short for Newton Trout, nothing complicated there—poked his head out into the alley. He was wearing his cook's cap and apron and had wrapped his bushy brown whiskers in a beard net.

"Hope ya'll are good n' ready," he said. "Everything's about set to go."

I turned to face him and started ticking off items on my mental checklist. "The turkey—?"

"Carved."

"The corned beef and pastrami?"

"Laid out on platters."

"The goulash . . ."

"Packed in a hot food carrier," Newt said. "Same for the stuffed cabbage and meatballs."

"Knishes, kugel, latkes, kasha varnishkes . . ."

"Them too. Plus we got plenty of supper rolls."

"Pickles?"

"Sours, half sours, you name it."

"And the sides?"

"I just got the lid down on a six-pound tub of coleslaw . . . it was so chock full I practically had to stomp it shut with my foot," Newt said. "Jimmy's crammed another one with potato salad."

I was feeling appreciative when panic struck. "The Sterno! Oh *crap*, I forgot to order the—"

"Watch your foul mouth," Thomasina interrupted. "When you gonna learn better'n to be vulgar?"

"Right, sorry, let's try this again," I said. "Oh Lawsy, Newt, this is a real bitch-stinker of a screwup. What in goddamned *hell* are we going to do now?"

He deliberately avoided looking in Thom's direction. "Don't fret. A.J. stopped by our wholesaler on her way into work, bought a whole carton of Canned Heat."

"Has anyone seen her yet?"

"She's waitin' in that fancy new convertible of hers." Newt jerked his chin toward the outdoor parking lot at our rear. "I asked one the bus boys to dig the warmin' trays outta the storeroom. He's gonna put them in her backseat so she can drive them over to the party."

Relieved, I exhaled through my mouth, the cigarette almost shooting from it like a dart from a ninja blowgun. "What about Medina and Vernon?"

"They already started out separate in Vern's rust-bucket."

I nodded. That would leave us seriously under-manned at the restaurant and force Raylene Sue Chappell, one of my best waitresses, to work the cash register. But I really didn't see an alternative. Lolo was plugged in to Nashville high society in a major way, and some of the city's most influential people would be among her guests that night. If word of mouth on our first catering gig was positive, there would be many more coming over the horizon.

"All right, Newt, I think we've covered everything," I said. "As long as you're okay with holding the fort tonight . . ."

"Don't you worry," he said. "We'll be fi—"

He broke off all at once, gawking at the van with his mouth wide open. I realized he hadn't yet noticed the logo on its side.

"Whoa . . . is it my imagination or are those letters supposed to look like slugs?"

"Worms," Thomasina said.

"Leeches!" Luke exclaimed inside the van. "Can't any of you folks *read*?"

Newt stared at him, his brow crinkling in disgust. "I stand corrected," he said. "I mean, leeches . . . they're gonna look a lot less nauseatin' when they roll in with our food, now won't they?"

\* \* \*

Four hours later, Thom and I were in the immense dining hall of Lolo Baker's restored antebellum plantation house, giving our buffet tables a final inspection. All pillars, porticoes, porches, gables and hanging eaves, the estate was set on three acres of farmland that had been in 's family for generations—or more accurately in her late husband Colton's family. It had been years, if not decades, since crops had grown in its fields, but Lolo didn't need their production in order to stay rolling in ripe green stacks of moolah. Thanks to Colton making some successful high-yield investments back in the freewheeling 1990s, she could afford to sit back and let the value of her financial shares grow . . . and grow and grow and grow. No watering, fertilizer, or plows required.

"Well now, it seems to me everybody's here," Thom said, looking up from a tray of beef goulash. The room's mahogany pocket doors had been slid back into the wall, giving us a wide open view of the parlor where Lolo's guests were having cocktails and hors d'oeuvres. "Another few minutes and they can come fill their faces before the stupidity begins . . . though I suspect some of the men might stay behind to get better acquainted with AJ's bra."

I didn't say anything. Once we'd hit the road, Thom had gone from griping about the party itself to the outfits we'd worn. I had prepared my responses in advance, figuring I was bound to hear her squawk about it at some point on the way out to Brentwood. And same as when I'd seen the band logo on the van, I frankly understood her exasperation—although I wasn't about to be latke batter to her hot oil and let her cook me till I was done.

Uncle Murray had wanted the atmosphere at the deli to be what he'd always called Western casual. As long as the staff dressed neatly he was satisfied.

But it was easy to distinguish diners from servers in a restaurant, where the customers stayed put at tables while the waiters and waitresses came around and took their orders. At special events, it was different. Because partygoers moved around and circulated, they had to be able to identify the servers in a crowd. That meant uniforms were a must.

I'd opted for basic black. Shirts and trousers for the guys, skirts and blouses for Thom, AJ and me, pairing them respectively with honey-gold silk neckties and feminine scarves of the same color and material. I told everybody they were free to choose their own footwear and tweak their outfits with whatever jazzy personal touches they chose, as long as they didn't stray from the color combo.

It still didn't go over well with the staff. Forget what I said about accents, they'd responded like I was forcing them into Sunday school outfits. And I admit their unhappiness surprised me. I didn't see what was wrong with wearing black. In fact, I thought it was kind of cool. Johnny Cash wore it. The E Street Band wears it. So does Angelina Jolie in *Lara Croft: Tomb Raider.* Well okay, I realize Angelina isn't much of a recommendation.

Anyway, after seeing how disgruntled they were,

I'd decided to set a positive leadership model in catering couture. Besides adding a wide retro patent-leather belt to my getup, I'd squeezed into a pair of black sky-high heels that made my feet look sexy, my legs longer, and my hips swingier . . . not to mention adding four or five sylphlike inches to my height. So what if they bunched my toes together like swollen red radishes? I'd had confidence in my ability to keep from screaming in pain till I got home and took them off. And bear in mind I *was* trying to prevent a full-scale staff mutiny.

Unfortunately AJ had pushed—or maybe I ought to say push-*upped*—the bounds of professional attire a little too far south of the modesty line, wearing her blouse half unbuttoned from the top, getting plenty of lift from the aforementioned bra, and guiding the eye down the Major Cleavage Expressway with a string tie straight out of a Dallas cowgirl pinup.

One thing, though. With the party barely underway my tootsies were already sore from rubbing together. And since that probably wasn't also true of AJ's twin peaks, I felt it was a little unfair for me to stand in judgment of their exposure level. Or stand, period.

I looked through the entry into the wainscoted parlor, where AJ was offering hors d'oeuvres to the guests, including a short, roly-poly man who was taking in a choice view of her personal scenery.

"The girl doesn't watch herself, she's gonna spill out into his food," Thom said. "That's *got* to violate some health code or other, Nash. Don'tcha think?"

I kept quiet. At first it was because I didn't want to spur her on. But then I realized I knew the man.

"Hey," I said. "That guy over there's Happy!"

"Sure does seem to be," Thomasina said. "Could a fella take any more time reachin' for his weenie-wrap?"

I frowned. Being the perennial church bakeoff queen of Nashville—I kid you not—Thom knew everybody's wife and mother and was consequently as plugged into the city's social scene as anybody. "Quit playing dumb. You know as well as I do it's Happy who owns the chocolate shop over on Fourth Avenue."

"Uh huh. And so what?"

"I just wouldn't have expected Lolo to invite him," I said, lowering my voice to a hush. "I'm not saying she's a snob. But most of her other guests *are* kind of upper crusty."

"And what makes you figure he ain't?"

I opened my mouth, then closed it, at a loss for words. In stark contrast to his deceptively, uh, happy name, Happy was a crude, unfriendly squeaker. He wouldn't part with an extra shopping bag if a customer begged and pleaded for one; it didn't matter that you were walking around his store with chocolates spilling from your arms and a sack of cabbages on your head. But I shouldn't have needed a reminder that the world was full of rich, cheap jerks. As a forensic accountant on Wall Street, I'd specialized in following the money trail of financial hotshots who were cooking their books.

I looked at Thom. "Okay," I said. "What's Happy's story?"

"Hapford's, you mean," she said. "His full name's Hapford Huttonson, Jr. 'Case that don't ring a bell, his dad was—"

"The ice cream king?"

"More'n that," she said. "He invented Hutton-son's chocolate patties."

*The ice cream sensation that looked like frozen cow patties*, I thought. For a while they'd even caught on big up north, especially among teens . . . or anybody with a juvenile sense of humor. "Wow, no *sh*—"

"Mind your cussin' tongue." Thom speared me with a reproachful glance, forget that I'd been speaking in a whisper. "Downtown rents and over-heads bein' what they are, ain't no way Happy could make ends meet sellin' candy bars."

"Are you telling me he's living off the family fortune?"

"Man's a trust-fund baby." Thom nodded, squar-ing her jaw. "The business doesn't turn a profit, he's always got his silent income to float it. That's how come he thinks he can treat customers the way he does. It's the same to him if he gets one or a hundred walking through the door every day."

I frowned and let that stand. Meanwhile, I wasn't too sure that *I* could go on standing much longer. My toes had cramped up something awful.

Thom noticed me shifting uncomfortably. "What's the matter?" she said. "You got quiet all of a sudden."

"So?"

"So quiet ain't your regular M.O."

I shrugged. Couldn't argue. "It's my feet. They're killing me."

She stared down at them. "Wah wah. I could've told you wearin' stripper shoes was a bad idea."

"Strip—Thom, these are dress pumps, *not* . . ."

She chopped her hand through the air to cut me off again, wiggling her foot to showcase her square-toed orthopedic flats. "Stop with the whiny excuses. Whatever happened to people takin' responsibility for themselves?"

I raised my eyes from the black bricks she was passing off as shoes and looked her in the eye. "I don't know. In fact, I'm waiting for you to tell me. And while you're at it, don't hesitate to explain what happened to you making sense."

"Should've expected that'd be your attitude," she snorted. "I worked hard my entire life. After thirty years in the restaurant business even my *bunions* got bunions. But you won't hear me cry."

I kept looking at her, caught by surprise. She seemed really aggravated and upset as opposed to being just her usual intentional pain in the neck. "Thom, what's wrong?"

"Forget it," she said. "I just don't appreciate people gettin' all judgmental about my choices or my footwear."

"Hang on . . . that's unfair," I said. "You're putting words in my mouth."

"You want to stick a label on me so you can feel superior, go right ahead and knock yourself out."

"I wasn't—"

Since there probably isn't much chance our squabble would have devolved into an out-and-out catfight, I won't exaggerate and claim we were saved by the bell. But we *were* interrupted by a glassy little tinkle from the parlor.

I turned toward the sound and saw Lolo Baker holding a brass dinner bell on the other side of the entryway. A slender, silver-haired woman in charcoal trousers and a paler-than-pale pink silk blouse, the mystery bash's hostess sported a pearl necklace with an appropriately detective-ish magnifying glass pendant and stood ringing the bell amid a lively crowd of guests.

"Excuse me, friends!" She beamed a smile. "Dinner will be served in ten minutes . . . and then our criminal mischief truly begins!"

Delighted murmurs around Lolo as Thom returned her attention to the goulash. She gave it a stir with her spoon, closed the lid, checked the burning Sterno underneath it, then sidled over to the tray of spinach-and-carrot stuffed flank steak.

A moment later she cocked her head at an angle, scrunched up her face like a puzzled bulldog, and began looking around the buffet table for something.

"What's the matter?" I asked.

"The gravy terrine," she said. "I don't see it anyplace."

I didn't either. But I did remember Luke carrying the gravy from our borrowed CreepLeeches van in its insulated container and promising he'd fill the terrine with it. "Hang on, I'll be back in a jiff," I said, and turned toward a hall giving off the dining room.

"Where you going?"

"The kitchen." We'd pulled our vehicles up around one side of the house to its entrance and lugged everything inside. Bet you the gravy's still there."

"All ri-i-ighteeo!" The drawling male voice, as well as the lip-smacking that went along with it, had come from right behind me. "I do so love to have nice, thick, piping hot gravy with my steak."

*Happy,* I thought, facing him unhappily. It hadn't been more than two minutes since Lolo's ten-minute dinner alert. "We're just finishing our preparations," I said, and struck my best professional pose. "Give us a few minutes and we'll have everything ready for you . . . and the rest of the guests."

I'd hoped Happy might take those last words as an unsubtle hint to scram. Instead he leaned forward to study the flank steak, then straightened with a cringe-worthy wink. "No tasters? For a good neighbor in the downtown business community?"

I stared at him. Putting aside that he'd never offered a penny's discount at his shop, it was the first time Happy had let on that he knew me from a hole in the wall. "How about I give you the same kind you give me?" I said.

Happy's mouth tightened. "Well, now, I can't quite recall—"

"Exactly," I said, swinging into the hallway.

The gourmet kitchen was at the end of the hall past a door to a storage or linen closet. I heard guitar playing from inside as I rushed closer and then saw Luke, dressed in a black Western shirt and matching skintight slacks, strumming away on his Gibson acoustic beyond the entrance.

"You mind if I ask what you're doing?" I said, stepping through.

He looked at me from where he stood beside a countertop. "I'm workin' out tonight's theme song, Nash."

"Theme?" I hesitated. "Newsflash, okay? This is a catered party. It is *not* one of your nightclub gigs."

I wasn't nearly old enough to be Luke's mom. But his baby blue eyes always brought out my maternal instincts. He smiled, all innocence. "I just figured that if we're gonna do these parties as a regular thing from now on, I could provide some special musical touches. Here, let me show you."

"Wait a sec, Luke. I need to find the—"

Too late. He was already plucking out a chord. And singing along to it. *"It's a deadly deli mystery, killer could be you, victim could be me. Time will tell, we'll have to see, what happens when the clock strikes three . . ."*

I held up a hand like a traffic cop. "Luke, please. Will you do me a favor and hit your *pause* button?"

He blinked a little woundedly and aborted the tune. "Sorry. I figured you'd love it."

"I, uh, do think it's very good." Talk about feeling guilt-tripped. "But it's way past three o'clock . . ."

"Right. That's how come I was smoothin' the kinks in here. I need a different word to rhyme with 'see'."

I cleared my throat. "Maybe we ought to discuss this later," I said. "At the moment I'm looking for the flank steak gravy. Have you seen it?"

Luke nodded and swung the guitar strap off his shoulders. Then he stood the instrument up against the counter and went over to a large stainless steel sauce pot on the range.

"I was warming it up while I composed," he said. "Ought to be about ready."

Ready or not, it was going out to the dining room. I spotted our terrine on the central kitchen island, hurried over to get it, ladled it full, and carried it toward the entryway, declining Luke's offer to take it himself. I was in too much of a hurry to start a fuss around.

That was when my foot seriously cramped up again. It was like a sadistic gorilla had my toes in its fist.

"Ouccchhhh!" I blurted.

"Nash, you all right . . . ?"

"Yeah, don't worry. Just put away your guitar and come help us in the dining room *pronto*."

I limped through the entry without waiting for a response. At least six or seven minutes must've passed since Lolo had waved her dinner bell in the air, leaving me with no time to waste.

I'd barely gotten into the hallway when I heard a loud crash over my head. And I mean loud enough to halt me dead in my tracks.

I looked up, the terrine in my hands. There was more crashing and pounding in what seemed to be the room directly above me . . . and whatever was causing it had made the ceiling visibly shake.

"What's *that* about?" Luke said. He'd raced to my side from the kitchen. "Sounds like some wild ol' chimp's jumping around upstairs."

I glanced over at him. It was a banner day for primate similes, I guessed. I was tempted to ask aloud if might be the same one that had mashed my foot.

I never had a chance to ask that or anything else. Before I could get out a word, or even react, we heard the loudest, most violent crash yet. And then the ceiling came down in front of us, breaking up into a dusty shower of plaster and lath and whatever else might've gone into two-hundred-year-old ceilings. I recoiled in shock and surprise, the terrine tumbling from my fingers, gravy spilling from it, splashing everywhere on the parquet floor. . . .

I suppose only an instant passed between the collapse event, as a police officer would call it later on, and the grisly arrival of Happy Huttonson through the hole above us. At the time I barely realized what was happening. I saw a big, wide body falling through the ragged hole, wondered in stunned confusion whether it actually *might be* an ape, and then recognized Happy as he reached the end of his downward plunge with a hard meaty thump, his arms and legs bent at impossible angles, one foot in a spreading brown puddle of gravy.

"Jeez," Luke said in a horrified voice. "Who's *he?*"

I stood looking down at the dead, broken body, dimly aware that the hallway had gotten crammed with partygoers. Most of those who hadn't fainted were screaming at the top of their lungs.

After a while I managed to pry my attention away from Happy and meet Luke's horrified gaze with my own.

"Guess it's pretty safe to say he's the victim," I replied at last.